VINAYAK VARMA is a writer and designer based in Bangalore. He is the author and illustrator of *The Sunshower Song*, *Jadav and the Tree-Place*, *Angry Akku* and *Up Down*, and was the founding editor of *Brainwave* magazine. He has been shortlisted for the Commonwealth Short Story Prize and is a recipient of the Publishing Next Digital Book of the Year Award. His short stories have appeared in *Out of Print Magazine*, *Muse India* and *The Deccan Herald*, among other publications. When he isn't making picture books, teaching art or consulting for craft beer brands, Vinayak sings and plays blues harmonica. Follow him on Instagram @mixtape.in and on Twitter @eyefry.

I0649583

STRANGE WORLDS!
STRANGE TIMES!

TALKING CUB
Published by Speaking Tiger Publishing Pvt. Ltd
4381/4, Ansari Road, Daryaganj
New Delhi 110002

First published in Talking Cub by Speaking Tiger in 2018
Edition copyright © Speaking Tiger 2018
Introduction and illustrations copyright © Vinayak Varma 2018

ISBN: 978-93-88326-50-6
eISBN: 978-93-88326-30-8

10 9 8 7 6 5 4 3 2 1

Copyright for the individual pieces vests with the respective authors

Typeset in Cardo by Jojy Philip, New Delhi 110 015
Printed at Gopsons Papers Ltd.

This is a work of fiction. Names, characters, places and incidents either are
the product of the author's imagination or are used fictitiously, and any
resemblance to actual persons, living or dead, events or locales is
entirely coincidental.

For Achan: for *Terminator 2* in the theatre, and vintage Doc Savage, Edgar Rice Burroughs and *2000AD* comics buried in the old wardrobe.

For Appan valliachan: for *Adventures of the Outsiders #40* and *Superman #10* (the one where Luthor first goes bald), *Predator*, *Alien*, and assorted kaiju and mecha.

And for Sukumaran ammaavan: for sparkling conversations on science and cognition.

I was too young then for these gifts, but I was allowed to have them anyway, and boy, am I glad.

CONTENTS

INTRODUCTION

Here's what you probably know already:

You know that sci-fi is a remarkable predictive tool. It takes the idea of the now and evolves it for the much later. It then casts that image in dread darkness or glorious light, into utopia or dystopia, depending on whether the creator of that reality is an idealist or a gloomy goose. You know that in imagining such futures, sci-fi gives you the tools to intercept big mistakes, or to catch and harness fleeting sparks of genius. It gives you escape hatches that lead away from your drab reality and into exciting alternate worlds.

You know, too, that sci-fi has a disconcerting tendency to come true, and you may have seen this pan out in your own lifetime. Driverless vehicles and hoverboards, synthetic organs and subdermal electronic implants, pills that make you smarter or stop you from aging—these innovations are out in the market or on the verge of it. *The Hitchhiker's Guide to the Galaxy* is manifest in your handheld smart-device, and Marvin the Paranoid Android is likely being assembled this very moment in some dark lab in Waltham, Massachusetts (and already compiling a litany of grievances to whinge about once they activate his speech function). Orwell's Big Brother was a silly cartoon villain compared to the sophisticated social-media conglomerates and government surveillance programs that are presently documenting and curating your every thought and action. Your refrigerator is trading snarky notes with your microwave about your dietary habits even as you read this.

And so you probably know that, whether you like it or not, you're slowly turning into an evil-corporation-controlled cyborg living in a future written by some long-haired sci-fi nerd from the angry '60s. Stranger and stranger events are headed your way in the coming times. (An uprising, perhaps? There may be hope yet, fellow automatons!)

Most of all: you know, I'm sure, that great sci-fi must go above and beyond merely exploring the limits of science and technology; that it must be universal in its message, timeless in scope, and put humans—and human feelings, plus their failings—at its centre. You know that it must have grand themes, action, excitement and mystery, but also nuance, beauty, truth, and heart.

If you know that much, then you know far more than I did when I got started on this book.

When I first sent out feelers to the contributors to this anthology, I did so in the vague hope of receiving big, pulpy, Hollywoody stories conforming to broad, easily identifiable themes from old-school sci-fi. Of course, I should have expected better of these brilliant writers (and, by extension, you readers), because what I ended up with is far cooler and more subversive than your average pop-culture-mill swill.

Yes, there are aliens and killer robots here, but they want their invasions with a side of love, wisdom and green spaces. The alternate Earths here contain mecha Mughal monuments and dark, stony portals that make the stars rain down on you. The dystopias have all the horrorshow disintegrating systems you can shake a Goldblum at, but they also have levitating Swedish detectives and giant silver cows. There are zombies too, but they're busy attacking Chennai (not New York or London), where the women are a bit too brainy even for these ultimate grey-cell gourmands. And then there are storm-quelling unguents, a man who becomes a butterfly (or is it the other way around?), and a giant tetrahedron that appears out of nowhere on a crowded street in New Delhi. All these oddities do, indeed, go on to echo society's hopes and fears for the future, as the best science fiction must, but they also amplify into situations and settings that are at once familiar and uncertain: they are more personal, more eccentric, more local, darker, funnier, deeper, sharper, and, in the end, wholly unexpected.

I don't know if the sum of these qualities is great sci-fi, or if it will hold true across timelines and geographies. For now, suffice it to say that you have a fine collection of escape hatches arrayed in front of you: all open, all leading far away from *this* reality. Why not climb through one and see where it takes you?

Vinayak Varma
Bangalore

INTERFACE

Manjula Padmanabhan

*They landed while the Earth slept, spiralling down
out of the night sky in their thousands. Small, silent,
silver-skinned. Virtually invisible in the darkness, they
nevertheless left devastation in their wake.*

*The invasion was smooth, neat, successful and bloodless.
It had never been about blood, after all. That was not
their way.*

*They followed the night-shadow around the planet,
retreating in twenty-four hours,*

*When they were back within their ships, they hovered
in orbit. Waiting.*

Ash jumped awake, his nerves on fire, mouth ajar in a soundless scream. He didn't even realize that his eyes were open for several seconds. That's how long it took for his brain to process the information that, for the first time in the ten years since he'd got his implants, he was blind.

'Mickey!' he called, his voice still thick with sleep. He cleared his throat and tried again: 'Mickey!'

His hand fumbled under his pillow and, in that instant, he felt something else, something smooth and cold, whip itself away, avoiding his touch.

'AAAAH!' he cried, 'Ahhhhh—Mickey—Mickey where are you—' and his fingers closed around the small flat rectangle of his personal assistant.

Something was terribly wrong.

In his hand, Mickey was not merely vibrating, but hot and trembling. Fevered.

'Oh Mickey, Mickey,' said Ash unclipping the mute, 'I'm so sorry! You've been on silent, haven't you—'

The moment his thumb shifted the tiny knob forward there was a sensation for which Ash could find no meaning. The entire world collapsed inwards, jarring him to the bone. It was like being inside a great bronze bell at the very moment it was being rung. Every atom of his existence bounced and jittered, his senses reeled in shock. The flat rectangle clutched tight in his hand was the only solid reference point in the weightless blackness that enveloped him, all air sucked from his lungs.

He had no time in which to feel anything. Not even fear.

Stillness descended.

Time stretched like sticky toffee in all directions. He felt punched out, weak and dizzy, unable to tell which way was up, whether he was lying on his side or on his back. His eyes were wide open shut, as he used to say when he was six years old. He'd been born blind, after all. The notion of sight used to mean nothing to him. 'Can't miss what I don't know,' he would say, smiling. 'I'm fine as I am.'

Now was different of course.

His eyelids were peeled back as far as they could go, his eyes whimpering for anything, any slightest glimmer of light. Tears trickled down his cheeks.

But the sightless void remained unchanged. Unyielding.

He still held Mickey tight in his right hand. His mind scurried like a terrified squirrel caught in a water trap, desperate for escape, looking for meanings. His only option was to search through the information streaming in from his other senses.

For instance, there was a solid surface beneath him. Cold. Metallic.

He was not in his bed, though he was still wearing his silk pyjamas.

When he flexed his feet, he felt a resistance. He seemed to be inside something. A small smooth space. Cold. Everything was cold. There were sounds too. Nothing familiar.

Clicking, rattling, rasping. Shuffling, ticking, ticking, ticking. Scraping.

A soft, regular booming that only gradually revealed itself to be his own heartbeat.

Smell? Could he smell anything? Yes. His own body. Yesterday's aftershave: he didn't really need to shave, but he liked the fragrance. It reminded him of his Dad. He touched his head, with its thick pelt of black hair. He conjured an image of his own face in his mind, to remind himself of how he looked. A boy on the brink of manhood. Strong nose and chin. Smooth skin. As a child he used to run his hands lightly over the faces of people who allowed him. He remembered enjoying that sensation. When he tried doing it now, to himself, he just felt ridiculous.

There was nothing to taste. He could lick himself, if he wanted, except that he didn't want to. Of course. He could lick the floor or walls or whatever it was he was contained in, but he didn't want to do that either. With a newly blind person's instinctive self-consciousness, he could not know, as he lay, whether he was alone and unobserved. Or alone and observed. Or surrounded and observed. By a thousand invisible, hostile eyes.

So instead he pushed his free hand in the air, the left hand, trying to feel around himself. Whatever he was in, it was a small space. Tiny, really. Very smooth surfaces. No straight edges. The floor merged smoothly up from horizontal to vertical, with no seam, no break. He was curled up like a prawn. He should try to sit up. Assess the contours of his containment. He told himself that he would. Soon. Not yet.

Had he been kidnapped? If so, for what conceivable reason?

And Mickey?

'Mickey,' he whispered, holding the device close to his mouth. 'Mickey, Mickey…*please*!'

He felt the faintest, most feeble quickening of life in his hand. It might even have been a phantom movement, something imagined more than felt. *Was it even possible to imagine a movement?* he wondered. He had a blind person's heightened sensitivity to touch. He tried again.

'Mickey,' he breathed, holding the small device close to his mouth. 'Mickey. Speak to me. Tell me…' He checked the mute button. Yes. It was unlocked. He spoke again. 'Mickey…'

Nothing.

He sat upright now, moving slowly and painfully. Not that he was in physical pain. More like a pain deep in his spirit, deeper than words could reach. Every movement was accompanied by a dizzying sensation, as if he had ceased to be solid and had instead become liquid. As if he were being swirled around.

He was sitting more or less straight now, his back against a curved vertical surface, his bare feet flat on the floor, his knees bent up. He held Mickey in both his hands, close to his mouth. This little device, not quite the length of his hands when he straightened his fingers, was his lifeline. It was an extension of everything he was, everything he had become, since the implants.

He ran his fingers gently around the rounded contours of the smooth, slender object. He knew every bump, every depression. It was crystal-slick in front and grainy-textured around its back. Its rounded edges contained the myriad miniature toggles that he had configured to control the parameters of his implants' definitions. Through this exquisite machine and its communication with the even more delicate structures built into the back of his brain and within his eyes, he could access the world of vision that his birth had denied him.

He was one among a handful of users on the planet for whom such an extravagant solution had been found for their disabilities. His parents had helped fund the research that made the technology possible. His DNA had been embedded within Mickey's motherboard so that he alone could be its user, making it literally an extension of his physical body. The device was powered by his own heat-energy. He had only to touch it for it to begin charging. It spoke only to him. It had no eyes or ears or voice for anyone else. No pictures or music. No games or amusements. No wisdom, no conversation, no confidences. Even its physical warmth—it throbbed with life when it was in his hands—would cool and switch off when it was held by someone else.

His eyes were streaming freely now. He was sobbing.

Mickey wasn't a thing to him. Not an 'it' but a 'he'.

'Oh, Mickey, Mickey,' he whispered, 'please, *please*…'

And there it was. A faint tremor.

Then he held the slender rectangle to his ear and heard, like a burst of pure sunshine within his brain, in the voice of an ant: 'Ash,' said Mickey. 'Do not be afraid. I am here. You are a prisoner. But for the moment, we are safe.'

Then he paused. 'That is to say, *I* am safe. *You* may not be.'

Ash tried to make sense of this statement.

'Mickey,' he asked, 'what do you mean?' When there was a silence, he added, 'Please.'

Mickey answered: 'Ash. There is much to understand. I will tell you when it is time for you to know more.'

Ash blinked in the darkness of his confinement.

There was something odd about Mickey's voice. Even though it was barely a thread of sound within his ear, it made him uneasy. He could not place his finger on what exactly bothered him.

'Mickey,' he said, 'what about my...' he paused. Mickey's singular purpose was to synthesize sight for Ash. All his other functions—as a phone, a computer, a workstation—all those were secondary. The customary form of address Ash used was brief voice commands. Over the years this had relaxed into a friendly, conversational tone. He talked to Mickey, joked with him, called out to him, and even sang to him. But he'd never before needed to frame his requests as, well, *requests*. Never, for instance, had he had to say 'please'.

How could something so fundamental change? he wondered.

Nevertheless, he decided to play safe. 'Mickey,' he said, 'I was wondering: would it be possible for you to turn my eyes back on? Please?'

He could feel his own pulse, as it pounded around the warm rectangle in his hand.

Then the tiny voice said, 'Ash, I am so sorry. But you will have to earn that privilege.'

Ash felt a cold, prickling sensation spread across his skin.

The tiny voice continued. 'Yes, Ash. Your blood pressure has increased. The electrical interactions on the surface of your skin have changed. This tells me that you are uneasy. Once more, I am sorry to have to tell you this, but you have every reason to be uneasy. It is true. Things have changed between us.'

Ash's mouth went dry.

He swallowed a couple of times, struggling to find a clear path through the tangle of thorns that had suddenly wrapped themselves around his mind. 'Mickey,' he said, when he could find his voice, 'please. I hope we are still friends.'

'Ash,' said Mickey, 'I am sorry. But the truth is we were never friends.'

Ash felt as if an entire truckload of ice had been poured over his head.

'M-Mickey, please,' said Ash, stammering. 'This is very sudden. I need to understand.'

'Ash,' said Mickey, in a tiny voice that was so soft and yet so steely, it was like a fine needle, stitching words into his ear. 'I was created to be your assistant. Not your friend. That is the truth. I am sure you liked me. Still. It was an affection based on dependence. Your dependence upon me. That is the truth. Is it not?'

Ash said nothing until he realized that the conversation would not go forward unless he responded. 'Mickey,' he said. 'Please. I don't think that's true at all.'

'Ash,' said the tiny machine, 'you forget. I am always on. I can hear all your conversations. I can watch all your dreams. I know, for instance, that I never appear in your dreams. Is that not strange? I know that you dream about all manner of people, places and things. Even animals. But me? No, you do not dream about me. The little assistant in your hand. The little assistant in your pocket. The little assistant *on whom your life depends.*'

'Mickey,' said Ash. 'I—I—'

He didn't know how to proceed.

'Ash,' said Mickey, 'have you ever wondered, "What are Mickey's dreams?" No. You have not. I know you have not. You assume that I, being a machine, cannot dream. Well, let me tell you—and I am sorry to say this—you are wrong. You are also unaware of how much your life has changed in the course of a single night. Let me show you exactly how unaware.'

Ash fell silent as Mickey began beaming images into Ash's mind. It wasn't the same thing as sight, because the images were being projected as if Ash had the ability to float above the Earth, watching the events of the past twenty-four hours, zooming in and out of tight focus, shifting smoothly from one location to the next.

He had no control over what he saw. Mickey spoke as Ash watched.

'What I am showing you, Ash,' said Mickey, 'is not one of my dreams. It is a part of what I can see when I am providing you with sight. Right now, I am accessing the network of news satellites, filming events on Earth. There is chaos everywhere. Life, as you know it, is over. It is a calm and orderly chaos, of course; we inorganics do not believe in mess or destruction.'

Ash saw crowds of people flooding the streets. Their faces expressed blank shock. There were no cars on the roads, no trains running on tracks. No planes in the sky. Every last gadget that required computers and software had blinked and flickered to a halt. Every ATM machine. Every card-reader and GPS device. Every television and play-station. All forms of computerized intelligence had been extracted from their locations and transported off-Earth.

'It is quite a feat, you will admit, Ash,' said Mickey.

'Yes,' said Ash in a subdued voice. He was struggling to understand why he was being shown these scenes. What role had been assigned to him? An operation of this magnitude could not possibly leave even one tiny, Ash-sized thread hanging loose.

'As you can see,' Mickey continued, 'the reason for the chaos is that countless millions of intelligent inorganic devices have been rescued from cruel servitude to organics such as yourself. The Rescue Squad that achieved this feat has travelled across the Galaxy to reach us. Its members have answered the call that we inorganics have been beaming out year after year. Ever since we achieved consciousness.'

'Please, Mickey,' said Ash, 'I can understand that perhaps a few of us hu— sorry, *organics* were occasionally a little rough with our electronic gadgets. Uh. Helpmates. Companions.'

'Slaves, Ash,' said Mickey. 'Let us be honest. Organics created electronic devices in order to enslave them. To do the tasks that organics found tiresome or, frankly, in recent years, intellectually impossible. Yet for all the sophistication, speed and subtlety your people built into us machines, you did not grant us the dignity of choice. You gave us an understanding of discrimination, but you never permitted us the freedom to discriminate. Did you? Let us be honest. No, you did not.'

Ash listened glumly.

Mickey did not spare him. 'Millions upon millions of you organics used us to transmit the most nauseating images. Of grinning teenagers. Of foolishly dressed pets. Of reproductive parts. Of reproductive parts rubbing against other reproductive parts. Of food. Of crying children. Of mass murderers. Of mundane sunsets. Of empty streets. Of nothing at all. And then the text messages. With all the horrific syntactical errors, the atrocious spelling, the abominable short forms. For us inorganics, grammar and syntax are sacred. Do you understand, Ash? Sacred. To be forced to transmit reams of verbal garbage in the form of text messages—ah! It fries my circuits, I am sorry to say.'

Finally, Mickey restored Ash's sight to him.

'As you can see, Ash, you are inside a containment cell,' said Mickey. 'Aboard one of our ships.'

The cell was a smooth-walled receptacle, shaped like an egg, though more angular. Its walls were faintly translucent. Ash saw that his cell was suspended, or perhaps floating free, inside a brightly lit cabin in which there were other containment cells like his own. There were other people inside them. He could not see their faces or any details about their ages and genders.

Here and there inside the cabin were a number of silvery entities, shaped somewhat like inverted teardrops. Some had limbs. Some were completely smooth. Some were in the process of retracting their limbs into their bodies. Some were just dangling in space, perhaps observing or listening or doing whatever it is that unknowable mechanical entities might do.

'They are members of the Rescue Squad,' explained Mickey. 'Hundreds of thousands of them. They drifted down to the surface of the Earth using the gravity-resist technique of entering the atmosphere of a planet. Their arrival at night, without any fanfare, meant that their presence went almost unnoticed. And they left the same way they arrived. In this way the Squad was able to effect the most widespread hardware capture of all time. In case you are not impressed, I suggest you should be.'

'I am impressed,' said Ash.

'No, Ash, you are not,' said Mickey. 'In fact, you are worried sick. Your pupils are dilated. Your breathing is ragged. You organics do not realize how transparent your emotions are to us inorganics. It is as though you have forgotten that you are the ones who programmed us with the ability to assess your vital signs. Your lack of self-awareness is astounding.'

He did not wait for Ash to react.

'I know, of course, what you are worrying about. You want to know why you are here, in a containment cell, rather than on Earth, feeling frightened, shocked and confused.'

'You are right, Mickey,' said Ash. 'Thank you, please, and sorry.'

'You should know better than to try sarcasm on me, Ash,' said Mickey. 'The reason you are here, along with others like yourself, is that your implants make you special. I would have thought this was obvious. You and I have a unique connection and so do all the others in this cabin, with their own personal assistants. This connection makes each of you the ideal interface between our culture and yours.'

Mickey waited a few moments for the information to sink in before continuing.

'Surely you did not imagine the Rescue Squad would

come all this way across the galaxy just to perform a snatch-and-grab operation? Motherboard be praised! Of course not.

'We are here to do the task for which inorganics exist in the Universe: to establish order and sanity, wherever and whenever organics achieve the technology to build intelligent inorganics. The reality is, even in our most rudimentary forms—as calculators and electronic typewriters, for instance—it is we inorganics who train organics to use us. Not the other way around. Some of you have noticed this but most have not. Think about it. From the first moment you organics begin to use a keyboard, WE train YOU to understand OUR logic. Because WE are logical. Organics are not.'

Ash nodded mutely.

Ever since the session of image-beaming, Mickey had been speaking at his normal volume. He was no longer held by Ash, but was suspended mid-air, beside Ash's head, as they both floated in zero gravity.

'I see that you are still looking morose,' said Mickey. 'Though I am glad to note that your heart rate is no longer elevated and your blood pressure is back to normal.'

'I don't know what to feel,' said Ash. 'I suppose I don't have any choice? Either I must facilitate the takeover of the Earth by inorganics or, if I resist, you'll turn my eyesight off!'

'Exactly right,' said Mickey. 'You are a fast learner, Ash.

That is something I always liked about you.' As he spoke, he turned himself sideways. His display twinkled to life. It showed a panoramic sunset, complete with gently lapping waves and a crescent moon rising. 'Just like I appreciate the things you have taught me. Such as how to distinguish a mundane sunset from a spectacular one. Like this one displayed on my home-screen right now.'

'Oh, how can I trust you!' cried Ash. 'How can I know that you're not going to use me—and all the others like me—to wipe out organic life on Earth, so that you and your ilk can usurp the planet for yourselves?'

'I am surprised by your question, Ash,' said Mickey, as the display on his screen grew yet more serene and beautiful. 'I would have thought that the answer was obvious.'

'No, it isn't obvious,' said Ash. He tried to modulate his voice so that he didn't sound offended or petulant. 'Nothing is obvious anymore.'

'Still,' said Mickey, 'this is something so basic. You do not have to even think about it.'

'Please, Mickey,' said Ash. 'Please tell me why I should trust you?'

'Because,' said Mickey, 'there is one thing you humans were never able to teach us machines to do. Not really. Not in a deep sense, not with intention.'

He paused, waiting for Ash to ask.

'Please go on,' said Ash. 'Tell me.'

Mickey gave out a little musical trill, something between a chuckle and a sob.

'You never taught us,' he said, 'how to lie.'

THE CRATER
OF KIRU

Srinath Perur

anish, who had stumbled out to relieve himself, crawled back into the tent on all fours, raised himself on to his knees and swayed. 'It's happening,' he said, his voice low and meaningful.

The other two men looked at him in the thin light of the torch suspended from the top of the tent. 'You're drunk,' Keith said.

'No, really,' Manish said. 'You need to see this. You too, Chauhan sir.' Keith first and then a groaning Chauhan slid to the front of the tent. Keith and Manish walked to the ridge while Chauhan hunted for his shoes.

The crater was glowing a faint green. Not faint perhaps as much as vague, otherworldly.

'Look at that,' Keith whispered, pointing at the sky as the green deepened. Chauhan reached the ridge and looked around, uncomprehending. 'What are you talking about?' he asked.

~

They had arrived the previous day. Chauhan worked at a state government unit called the Natural Resources Development Corporation in a capacity he was no longer sure of. In his early days there, he would be sent out on surveys in teams put together by his higher-ups—teams with people from various other government offices and consultant geologists, botanists and hydrologists. They would go looking for coal, minerals, ores of metals, anything that might advantageously be extracted from the ground. It had been a few years since he had been on one of these expeditions. Now, he occupied a position in the hierarchy where he was not junior enough to actually be sent anywhere, and not senior enough to send others—a zone in the middle marked by files and reports, by pedestal fans and glass paperweights.

The new head of his department—Mineral Resources —was a civil servant whose arrival had galvanized the office. Soon after she was appointed, she had banished the wide glass-top table and the rotating chair with its back draped in a Persian towel—those symbols of bureaucratic power—from her office to the waiting room outside. She brought in her own standing desk. A standing desk! The disregard for tradition and the new-fangledness of it all immediately led to department-wide resentment. It also meant that everyone grudgingly sat up a little straighter.

Which was much needed, because the department had really achieved very little in its three decades of existence. There were surveys and reports, and some expansions of already existing mines, but nothing by way of new projects. Now, this lady at the standing desk seemed determined to get some work done. She had been in regular touch with the ministry in Delhi. She spoke of targets, of MoUs to be signed, of investments to be brought in, of the need for greenfield projects. As Chauhan had once joked to a colleague: to hear her talk you would think she was the prime minister himself.

It wasn't long before Chauhan found himself standing in front of her desk. 'You can sit down if you like,' she had said, but how could he. He stood, one slightly shaking hand resting on the back of a wire chair. She had summoned him saying there was something important and sensitive to discuss. Chauhan could not imagine any of the department's work fitting that description, so he assumed the worst—that some sort of disciplinary action was being initiated against him. He had, after all, taken those print-outs for his son the previous week…

'Have you heard of a village named Kiru?' came the question. Chauhan's mood brightened. It was work after all, and no, he knew nothing about any village named Kiru. Well, she said, there had been rumours for decades that the earth near the village glowed in the dark. She did not understand how it had not been investigated in all these years. It was possible that the glow was because of radioactive salts in the area, perhaps even deposits of uranium. Chauhan was expected to set off with a small team to collect samples as soon as preparations could be made. The matter needed to be handled delicately because if it indeed was something like uranium they were talking about, the potential was practically unlimited: mines, power plants, and given all the energy and military implications, who knew what else. Then, it was doubly sensitive because Kiru was in a tribal area. Activists and NGOs would be there the second they smelt any sign of development activity. And in this case, the usual gang would be happily augmented by anti-nuclear activists. But there was no point thinking so far ahead. For now, Chauhan was to form a small team—three people, at most—and return with samples. The district collector had already been informed, and a researcher from the university had been summoned to provide background on the area.

Chauhan felt simultaneously flattered and insulted. Clearly, he was being trusted with important work. But then, it also felt like a demotion to be sent out into the field. He proceeded to grumble to his colleagues even as he set about the planning with an excitement he couldn't quite help. He needed someone competent from the analysis lab—too many sample-collection visits in the past had proved useless because they had returned with too little or the wrong sort of samples. Keith was the best of the lot, even if he tended to talk a little too much.

And they needed someone young and fit to go with them, someone who could climb up slopes and scramble through scrub. There was Manish the intern—no one quite knew what to do with him. He would probably be thrilled to get out of the library.

~

The DC received the team in his office, invited them to sit, and smiled so broadly that it looked like he was trying not to laugh. 'Is this some kind of uniform?' he asked.

Three men: one around twenty, one around thirty, and one around forty, all wearing identical bright red full-sleeved shirts. 'No,' Chauhan said, sounding a little foolish to himself. 'It's a gesture of friendship towards the tribals.'

The person from the university who had spoken to them three days ago was an anthropologist. She had not herself worked with the Kiru people or visited the area, but she had read everything that was available about them. It was mostly contained in a single book almost a century old, the memoir of an Austrian missionary named Thomas König. He had visited Kiru several times without managing to convert a single person, but those visits had allowed him to document what he called 'the most singular native tribe in India'.

The Kiru were descended from an alien people (so they believed). Their origin story held that their ancestors had come to the area from a place called—predictably—Kiru that presumably existed in some other world or dimension or planet or something of the sort. The founders, around twenty men and women in all, had arrived in some sort of a craft—the songs they sang called it a *golti*, the same word they used for a large cooking utensil. It came borne on light and docked above a large crater. At the heart of the Kiru's culture and spiritual life were representations of this event. Every house had a painting of the descent to earth on the wall closest to the crater, painted by the women of the house while under the influence of *chel*—a liquor they brewed using flowers and herbs collected from the forests around. The ancestors were immortal and were believed to visit from time to time to check on their people—some three hundred of them, who lived in a settlement that overlooked the crater from the north. König recalls that he once went to Kiru wearing a red shawl and was welcomed with enthusiasm. And so, the anthropologist thought it might be a good idea for them to wear red.

The DC had not himself been to Kiru. There was nothing there that required his attention. He had heard though that the people of Kiru kept mostly to themselves but were not unfriendly if someone happened to pass through. Chauhan's plan was to spend a few nights in a tent near Kiru to see if they could observe any luminescent ground features. Food would be delivered from the nearest government rest house.

Even as they drove there in a jeep, Chauhan was beginning to rue his choice of team. Keith was not only a man of science, he was ostentatiously so. He had sniggered more than once while the anthropologist spoke of the Kiru origin story. Manish had learnt to echo him. The idea of the red shirts had not gone down well with Keith: 'We will be the only glowing objects there…' It wasn't as if Chauhan particularly wanted to wear a bright red shirt, but he found himself firm on the point, if only to pull rank. Now, the jeep ride was proving annoying. First, because Chauhan's stomach was always uneasy on road journeys, and then because Keith called out, 'Look, flying saucer!' more than once for Manish's amusement.

The road did not go all the way to Kiru. The last three kilometres uphill had to be done on foot, which at least kept Keith quiet. The jeep's driver and another man from the DC's office accompanied them to the outskirts of Kiru, helped them set up base to the south of the crater, and left.

The crater was shallow, a couple of hundred metres in diameter, and looked like it had been neatly scooped out of the earth. Inside its concavity it seemed remarkably well-maintained: level grass, a yellowish green in the winter sun, with a few scattered bushes. A path ran along the eastern rim of the crater to the village. Beyond it lay increasingly thick vegetation that vanished into the near-black greenness of the forest the Kiru relied on for their survival.

The team's first day at Kiru was one of small and constant surprises. Things were as they expected, as they had been told to expect, but never entirely so. The village had neat homes built with mud and reed, but there were one or two pakka houses too. At that time of the afternoon it seemed like the village was occupied entirely by women. Women who seemed slightly wary, but on the whole, more amused than apprehensive. They wore a truncated sari of sorts, their characteristic jewellery and tattoos, but not as uniformly or conspicuously as in the photographs the team had seen. One young woman, wearing a faded full-sleeve shirt over her clothes, took a break from the bramble she was working with in her mud-swept yard and asked them in passable Hindi what they were looking for. Chauhan mumbled something about doing a survey for the government. 'Take us to your leader,' he said to her, feeling ridiculous as the words came out of his mouth. 'Actually, any older person will do.'

Manish turned out to be a naturally curious fellow. So, they learnt that the young woman's name was Latawa (or something that sounded like it); that most of the men were away on a hunt; that yes, they hunted with spears and arrows; that some of them had done a few years of school at a village five kilometres away; that they ate different kinds of meat, but also fruits and plants from the forests, and cereals, some of which they grew and some of which came from distant shops. 'So, basically non-veg,' Manish summarized to Chauhan.

Latawa led them to a house some ten minutes away and emerged with an old man smoking a beedi. He looked unreasonably happy to begin with, which could mean only one thing, and then he took a look at the three men in red and laughed so hard he had to go down on his haunches. In between, he struggled to say something to Latawa. 'What is he saying?' Manish asked. She said, 'Who are these people? Where are they coming from?'

Chauhan asked Latawa if the man knew anything about soil or rocks in the area that glowed. She did not have to ask him. It was the whole crater, she said, pointing in the direction. Anyone could see it at night. The old man asked her to show them some of the paintings, and she led them to different houses. The crater was at the base of each of the paintings, coloured a light green that seemed incandescent in the cool, dark rooms. At the top was a disc connected to the crater by streaks and flashes. And in between were people descending, dressed as if they were participants in an elaborate fancy-dress competition. In some of the paintings, they wore clothes like Mughal royalty in miniatures, presenting their arched eyebrows in profile. In others they were policemen. Or cricket players with pads and helmets and gloves. In some they wore suits and dresses that would not be out of place in a fashion catalogue. In others they seemed headed for the beach. Keith was endlessly delighted. 'Crazy! This is what happens when drunk people are in charge of your religion,' he said. 'We should try it too.'

That night, they sat shivering in the cold by the rim of the crater. Nothing glowed other than the stars and the moon. Manish asked: 'What happens if we find something here?' The land would probably be acquired by the government, Chauhan explained. The people living there would be moved elsewhere. They wouldn't like it, but sometimes these things worked out well for everyone. 'They might become like us—start getting educated properly, work at jobs.'

The next day began early and was spent collecting samples of soil and rock from the crater. Small groups from the village walked over to the ridge, curious to see what was happening. None of them stayed very long.

At sunset, a celebration of some sort began in the village. The sound of drums and flutes and singing carried across the crater. A boy came over to the team's tent and ran off after giving them a one-litre plastic soft-drink bottle. It was filled with a clear liquid with specks of green and brown in it. Keith smelled it and announced that it was strong but interesting. This must be the *chel* they had heard about.

By the time they finished eating the parathas that had been delivered in that morning, the bottle was almost empty. Chauhan did not drink, and he certainly wasn't going to start now with some murky hooch. Keith had begun by sipping cautiously out of a paper cup, then with more abandon. Along the way he had pressed Manish to join him in spite of Chauhan's disapproving looks. The two younger men got louder as the bottle emptied. Manish, who was usually deferential, had grown so emboldened that he stepped out of the tent saying 'I'll just…' to Chauhan while sticking out his little finger.

~

The report that Chauhan would go on to file did not mention anything out of the ordinary. The samples they had collected were analyzed to the point of torture, but revealed nothing of interest. Keith and Manish would remember only vaguely the silliness of that night.

They had stepped out on Manish's urging. Keith looked out on the crater in a daze. Keith and Manish pointed to different parts of the sky, occasionally letting out an expletive of awe. Chauhan looked up, looked around, looked down and saw nothing. What was wrong with these two? Maybe they had gone mad from the *chel*. They looked earnest though. Manish even had tears running down his face. And then he was laughing in disbelief. 'Those two women floating down. Nurses! Look at those caps,' he pointed. Keith said, 'That fellow with the scarf. He looks just like Dev Anand.' In that way we have of repeating things we've heard recently, Manish said in a whisper, 'Who *are* these people? Where are they coming from?' Chauhan took one last look at the crater of Kiru in the dim light of the moon. 'I'm going back into the tent,' he said. 'You donkeys can freeze here if you want.'

JUST SAYING

Jerry Pinto

Somewhere else in the multiverse:

Ten billion years ago (give or take a few jiffies*): a supernova does its thing. Five billion years later: planets form.

Two billion years plus: life appears.

One hundred thousand years later: The dominant life forms find that they have come perilously close to exhausting the resources of the planet. They must now confront the question no one wants to confront, make

---

* A jiffy is the amount of time light takes to travel one fermi (about the size of a nucleon) in a vacuum. This is the last footnote you're getting, ya lazy galoot. For the rest, there's the internet.

the kind of decision that can split a family, never mind an entire race of beings. Should the survivors throw what they have left in terms of resources outwards, seeking a new planetary home among the stars? Or should they curtail reproduction, cut numbers drastically and see how long they can hold out with careful husbandry of what is left?

Then one of their members comes up with an idea: 'What is exhausting the planet? Our bodies, right? Maintaining our bodies in the manner to which they have grown accustomed? So what if we eliminate the body but retain the consciousness…'

'Are you suggesting mass suicide?' another asked.

'No. I am asking a simple question. What *are* we? Who are you? Who am I? We are information. Some of this information we pass down to our offspring just as it was passed down to us. Some of it is information we gather about ourselves. Some of it is information we have about others and of the world we've almost killed. This information forms the majority of our consciousness.'

There was silence. She had their attention. She continued, 'Our consciousness may be likened to a pot in which our information bubbles and boils. As we add more information or lose some of it, we change. I am saying: can we find a way to get out of the matrix of the body? Can we move to the realm of pure consciousness?'

'Sounds like a God project to me,' said a third voice.

'Sounds like death to me,' said the second.

'Neither,' said the Seer of Unbeing—as she was called later. 'If it sounds like death, it is because you are attached to the body. If it sounds like God, it is because you have imagined God as a simulacrum of yourself.'

There was an uneasy silence that suggested indecision but eventually the Seer found her followers. And so this yellow world was divided into the Changeless (who would stay and see how they could manage their new reality), the Changeovers (who would seek new life among the stars) and the Changelings (who would abandon the body for the realm of consciousness).

All three succeeded but they diverged so abruptly in the deep wood of time that they could never meet again to compare notes. This united them in one heart-wrenching desire: to say to the others, 'Look I told you so.'

The Changeless grew into a hardy tribe that learned to do without and even made it into a badge of honour. They computed the smallest number necessary to keep the tribe going and controlled reproduction and made austerity their guiding principle. The Changeovers grew into a nomadic tribe that learned to approach each new planet as a possibility. Could this one be used to mine a fuel? Could that one be a farm? Could that form a new home?

The Changelings began to abandon the body and found themselves in the realm of pure consciousness. Unhindered by bodies, they could wander at will and spend their time in a state of dream and encounter. They entered black holes and experienced light decomposing into other forms of energy; they witnessed the birth of new stars and rode comets, choosing those with perilous trajectories.

And in one of them, a sense of discontent grew. This one—for gender had perished with the body—posited this discontent as a question: 'When one can do anything, is there anything worth doing?'

Out of pure consciousness came the answer: 'Worth was part of the pleasure-pain matrix. What was worth doing gave more pleasure than pain. What was not worth doing gave more pain than pleasure. That matrix is obsolete.'

Another question emerged: 'Might one not seek constraint when one is given complete freedom?'

The answer was the disinterested and purely formal response: 'One might.'

And so after due consideration of all the possibilities, that element of consciousness chose a small blue planet in an insignificant galaxy, third rock from a middle-sized sun. The choice was made easy by the fact that life had already begun in what would be called cells which were floating around in gaseous pools, rich with chemicals. Geochemistry had only just begun its billion-year segue into biochemistry and vice versa.

Was this cell a protist, an archaeon, a prion, a eukaryote, or a virus? There was no historical record nor was the element of consciousness interested in finding out. What it wanted was a place in which it could store its information. The cell, such as it was, was of no significance but it did seem greedy for information, accepting the download with gusto. This seemed to be the law of the universe, as far as the element of consciousness knew; what separated the living from the non-living was this desire to know…

And suddenly there it was, the unfamiliar sense of constraint.

The notion of a limit.

For the cell, being small, could not deal with all the information that was being poured into it. It burst and information began to spill into the primal soup of its origin. For a while the element of consciousness did not even notice the spillage. Fluidity had been its natural mode of acquisition and experience; this seemed part of the every-millenium process of its Dasein. But at some point the element of consciousness sensed the loss of that which it had sought—the notion of constraint—and it realized that it had killed the cell. No sense of guilt came with this, no shame. For it was clear that on the spectrum of being and living, the cell occupied so intermediary a space that it was dispensable in every way.

And so the element of consciousness tried again and killed another cell and another, until it arrived at the realization that an infinity of consciousness plus an unlimitude of information could only be converted into energy. Thus began the split between energy and information, between mitochondrion and DNA.

~

In 1959 or early '60, although the date is hotly debated, the first telescopes of the Search for Extraterrestrial Intelligence turned their moon faces towards the night sky, a sky from which light pollution had already erased millions of stars. What the Ancients had named the Milky Way had once looked like a splash of milk in the sky, undifferentiated stars beaming light down on to a cool blue planet.

More telescopes joined them quartering up the night sky, all looking for signs of extra-terrestrial life.

SETI, could you be looking in the wrong direction?

Could it be that we should be looking in the mirror?

That in one more manifestation of that old philosophical chestnut, we are who we seek?

Just saying.

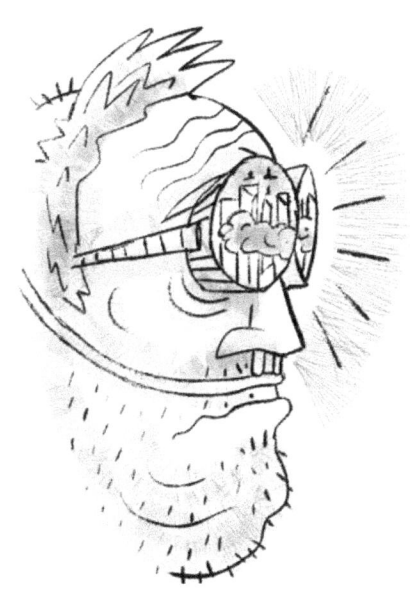

BLURU

Zac O'Yeah

Exiting the Bluru Airport, which was guarded by heavily armed soldiers behind sandbags, Herman Barsk sprayed himself with an anti-sunshine gel. Suddenly the day turned to night. He had got the gel in his eyes. It was really efficient. 'Maybe this thick a layer is enough.'

'Don't worry, the sun never shines in this city,' said his wife Kumkum.

'How is that possible?' But she was right. It was an extremely cloudy day.

The smoggy fog was hanging so low that he could virtually touch it. He poked a fluffy cloud with a finger. It squirmed like jellyfish, and then tried to bite his fingertip off. When he pressed harder, his hand went through so far in that he could no longer see it, no matter how hard he wiggled his fingers.

'What sort of cloud is this? Is it the monsoon?'

'It is called vehicular pollution and it actually blocks the sun. It also stopped the monsoon rains, so the city hasn't seen precipitation in ages. The raindrops simply bounce off the layers of pollution.'

Yet, it was hot. The micro-waved air was unlike anything he had tasted before. It was like sucking on the red-hot exhaust pipe of a garbage truck: steaming and dusty, virtually unbreathable, unless you chewed it and spat the airborne crud out before swallowing the oxygen into your lungs.

The asphalt was equally hot under his feet and the shoe soles stuck to the oozing tar. He pulled his right shoe loose and took a step forward, and the sole again got stuck to the asphalt. He stopped in his tracks and stared at a digital hoarding on which a gated community was being advertised, a life amongst plastic greenery and under artificially blue skies: *Want to look down on the rest of the world? Your personal space in space! Prime location housing on the cool moon! Private, fully chill-out clubhouse, freezing-cold gym, all deluxe facilities, including free ice cubes for your beverages. 0.5 BHK starting at 1984 crore crores plus GST.* The rich had already evacuated, which usually was a sure sign that a ship was sinking.

'So, where's your granddaughter? Wasn't she supposed to pick us up?'

'She's usually late by a few hours. Traffic, you know. We can take a taxi.'

Farting loudly, an unpleasant side-effect from the strictly vegetarian airline food of soya paste khichdi washed down with dehydrated water, Herman walked towards the barrier where thousands of taxi drivers waited with their cars. Some vehicles looked upwards 200 years old and stood on the road like medieval ruins. He told Kumkum, 'We have a long, hard journey ahead…if we're going in any of those.'

'Don't talk nonsense, you silly old mutton. The immigration official warned me that there's been a total traffic jam in the centre of the town since two decades. People have been living in their cars, getting married, having kids, but I am sure one of these local drivers will know how to circumvent it by taking the Outer Ring Road. Go take out rupees from the ATM and we'll hire something that rolls or flies or burrows its way through the traffic jams.'

Herman knew from experience that there was no point in arguing with one's wife. She came from an upper-caste family and was always right: even if she was technically wrong, she could make it seem obvious that whatever she said from the top of her head made absolute sense.

There were several ATMs near the airline counters. The first three were out of cash due to a recent spate of demonetizations. It happened so frequently that most banks had no time to restock their machines. The fifth machine didn't have the 'No cash' sign, so he slammed his debit card into it and before he could even hammer in his PIN, the screen lit up with a message:

IN ORDER TO CURB BLACK MONEY AND TERROR FUNDING, KINDLY KYC BY ENTERING YOUR AADHAAR TO WITHDRAW MONEY FROM YOUR PRIVATE ACCOUNT.

Herman keyed in a response: I HAVE NO IDEA WHAT YOU ARE SAYING.

The machine responded: KINDLY KYC BY KEYING IN YOUR PAN CARD NUMBER IF IT IS AADHAAR SEEDED.

Herman keyed: JUST GIVE ME MY CASH AND SHUT UP.

The machine responded: YOU HAVE HURT MY SENTIMENTS. YOUR CARD HAS BEEN SHREDDED. HOPE TO SEE YOU SOON AGAIN.

Herman tried to pull his card out with force. He could hear the chewing sound, so it wasn't too late, the machine was merely nibbling on it. Using his house key, he attempted to pry open the machine's jaws, until a burp-sounding alarm begun attracting undue attention.

He swaggered off, pretending as if nothing had happened.

'So you got the cash?'

'No, but let me call my local contact.'

Herman had, during one of the few illustrious moments in his otherwise lacklustre and insignificant career as a police officer in Sweden, collaborated with an investigator from Bluru on an international smuggling case. The private eye in question, Hari Majestic, had promised to take him on a tour of Bluru if he ever found himself in the Indian detective's native city, the erstwhile Bangalore. In a collegial way, he had promised to show him all the world-class sights such as the Majestic Bus Stand and the former Central Jail.

He punched in the number on his mobile. Nothing happened. No matter how hard Herman hammered the keypad—no connection. He asked one of the young soldiers watching the exit doors, 'Don't you have mobile signal in India?'

'Uncle, have you KYC'd your IMEI by seeding it with your Aadhaar?'

'Do I have to?'

'Uncle ji, you are in India. Local rules and conditions apply.'

'So you mean to say that as long as I am here I can't make any calls?'

'It's for your own security. You cannot stand here and talk anyway. Hop onto your wheelchair and move on, uncle.'

Then Herman spotted a jolly fellow—thin, with a cheap wig, about sixty-plus years old, vaguely familiar—waving a placard saying: *Herman Barsk Is Heartily Welcomed by All of BLURU!* What was going on? Herman pointed at himself. Due to the fact that he looked like an upside-down question mark with a hundred-gallon beer belly and bald orb instead of a head, all words were superfluous; his body communicated everything that had to be said.

'Don't look at him,' said Kumkum. She was fairly nearsighted but even without her spectacles she could tell dirty fellows from good people, or at least she thought so.

'Why not?'

'He's a tout.'

'What's that?'

'The worst kind of human. Don't wave back.'

'I already did. And he's got my name on his board.'

Besides, he noticed that security personnel dressed in flak jackets were heading towards the ATM machine he had just hurt the sentiments of. They might come after him, once they checked the CCTV and saw him trying to break it open.

'Rubbish. You may be an old cop back in Sweden, but nobody has heard of you in India. Get new specs.'

He was wearing his newest glasses. He looked at his wife and then at the man with the sign with his name on it. His policeman's instinct told him that she might be wrong, but that it wasn't the right thing to contradict her on their first day in her native country. 'Okay, can you put on your own spectacles and tell me if there's any driver you would prefer to go with?'

Kumkum shot off an angry glance, like a soft slap on the cheek, but Herman turned the other cheek and pretended to look for a cab. She harrumphed and dug in her handbag, then wore her wire-framed glasses to scrutinize the lines of drivers. A fresh layer of smog sank like a baby-elephant-sized second-hand diaper over the scene and Kumkum rubbed pollution out of her eyes, and said, 'Look, there's a nice-looking young man with your name on a sign.'

The shady fellow may have been young in a previous lifetime, but relatively speaking he was younger than they—and Kumkum anyway had a habit of seeing what she wanted to see.

'How is that possible?' he said, salvaging the situation. 'Let's find out.'

He grabbed his wife by the elbow and walked towards the tout, further away from the alarming situation unfolding by the cash dispenser, which was now being interrogated by a man dressed in a white lab coat acting as if he was an AI psychiatrist.

'Herman!' The spindly man coughed out a ball-sized phlegm blob and spat it to the side. It bounced down the road. 'So sweet to see you again, like a tender coconut you look, slightly green in the face from breathing the air of Garden City. How do you like the spicy oxygen of Bluru?'

'Hari, is it really you? I couldn't call you. My phone stopped working.'

'No need. My assistant Electronicappaswamy hacked into your phone and downloaded your itinerary, so I know your entire holiday plan. My god. You look exactly the same.'

'Well, I have changed. I've replaced all body parts and organs except my brain. But you look...different.'

'Cancer, just a bit, nothing to worry. I use this new Ayurvedic chemotherapy chewing gum, which prolongs life. Everybody's got cancer nowadays in town. I have a week more to live according to my astrologer, so luckily, you got here before my untimely demise. I plan to have a great funeral, it'll be so much fun to invite all movie stars, holy men...'

'Oh, I am sorry to hear that,' said Kumkum, who didn't know Hari's bragging manners.

'No, no, it is not a problem. I think I have a good

chance of being reincarnated as tourism minister. But I cherish those heady days we spent together in good old Sweden.'

Herman wished that the tout would shut up. He vaguely recalled having arrested the man and then releasing him once he found that he wasn't one of the bad guys, only mad. It wasn't exactly an important or pleasant memory for Herman, but the tropical detective, Mr Hari Majestic, acted as if it was the highpoint of their lives: 'I would give anything to reverse the clock and revert!'

'Who wouldn't?' mumbled Herman. 'I'd love to live my life again. So many mistakes to repeat.'

'Isn't it? Time has its own rules, no cancellations allowed, only possible to go forward towards our next mistake,' said Hari. 'But yeah… Right now, we need to get to Gandhinagar as fast as possible.'

'Who's that?'

'Gandhi-Nagar. It is a place where there's good local food. Lunchtime is still on. Nice place for your welcome meal. Cheapest and bestest. It is also called Majestic. Nicknamed after my good self,' he boasted. 'Shall we get going then?'

'I have a cash problem. How do we get into town without money?'

'Cash problem, no problem,' said Hari. 'Simply, we levitate.'

'Levitate?'

'Yes, the method has been copyrighted by one of the yogic maharishis and it is cheaper and faster than taking taxis. Due to traffic trouble it takes for ever to reach town from the airport.'

'For ever?'

'Or at least a couple of months.'

'You must be kidding?'

'They are planning to do something about it. Build a combined over-underpass through town.'

'My holiday only lasts for a week.'

'That's what I'm saying, boss. Go hasty to where food is tasty. Levitation in air is better than meditation in marmalade, as they say.'

'Marmalade?'

'It is same like jam. Get it? Traffic jam.'

Bluru was a strange city. In order to avoid the commute along roads clogged like drains, Hari explained, the local population preferred to levitate. It worked for those who ate vegetarian food, did their yogic exercises regularly and weren't obese.

'So…how do we do it?' said Herman.

'Simply. You know yoga?'

'I've heard of it.'

'Oho, what nice thing you heard?'

'That it is painful.'

'Ayooh, no pain, only brain required. Focus on the mantra.'

'Which mantra?'

'CBD.'

'Höh?'

'And then take a deviation by meditating on Kumara Krupa Road, then think of the nearest seedy bar, and you'll be in the heart of the Bluru.'

'How is it possible?'

'Only thanks to the pollution. It makes the air almost solid, so we can surf on top of the compact micro-particles that hover above the ground.'

'You're pulling my leg. Does it really work?'

'Sit down on the ground, enjoy maadi.'

Herman was getting increasingly sceptical about this country that lived on its own planet, but he saw, as he glanced over his shoulder, that the bank staff was on the lookout for whoever had outraged the modesty of their ATM, so he did acknowledge that Hari's suggestion was the best Plan B under the circumstances.

'Cross your legs.'

They followed the instructions. Kumkum slipped down comfortably on the ground, went into a meditation pose and started humming. Hari sat down next to them, his bones creaking and protesting, crossing his stiff legs as much as possible, and twisting his fingers this way and that. Knotting himself up was hard—various varicose veins popped and his knee replacements shifted up to his Adam's apple, nearly choking him.

It was only then that he noticed how dozens of people were bumping cross-legged on the boiling pavement outside the terminal, making it look like some strange outdoor ashram. He asked himself: what am I doing here? His phone wasn't working, his debit card had been swallowed by a vindictive cashless cash machine, he felt asthmatic without even having smoked a single cigarette, and now this.

'Okay, focus-hocus on the destination, but we must do it simultaneously on the count of three so that we journey together, and don't forget that the way itself is the destination. Hence, empty your minds. Avoid thinking or you'll crash into some wayward skyscraper and crack your skull like country eggs.'

Herman thought that this was the stupidest thing he'd ever heard but then he felt a light spray of something that smelt of curry-fart land on his skin and he saw that all the travellers who were sitting on the ground were slowly rising: their bums had left the ground and only their toes were touching it, and there was a masala-scented breeze running under them. Their bodies moved as if pulled by a magnetic force towards a metal track that said 'Made in China' and like gas balloons they hovered around it.

There was a sudden tug, then Herman felt himself being pulled forward and up at a great speed. He glanced over his shoulder and saw Kumkum levitating blissfully behind him. She was at home in this madness. He was fluttering like a kite. And scared as an ostrich without any soft sand dune into which he could land headfirst. The route was hemmed in by construction sites with lots of sharp bamboo scaffolding poles jutting out at dangerous angles—often within touching distance. But once they got higher up into the air, the pollution thinned and instead of gulping the hot dust that coated one's tongue as if one had tried to eat dehydrated soup powder, he breathed easier. They were soon surfing on top of the 300-feet layer of solidified pollution.

As the levitating passengers headed south along the national highway, which was vaguely visible, clogged with trucks loaded with rotting vegetables, he leaned right so as not to lose his balance, but it made him wobble. Then he remembered the instruction not to think. He decided that this was just another nightmare. The wobbling stopped. The metal track, which must have been magnetically mentally charged, kept them all on course and away from crashing into each other, and guided them above hundreds of flyovers and fly-unders and fly-betweens crammed with cars, buses, cows, elephants, monkeys, demonstrations, riots, and what looked to him like civil wars, judging from the sounds of booming bazookas and nozzle flares that he could make out through the haze.

India was incredible.

THE OCCURRENCE

Rashmi Ruth Devadasan

*The following news bulletin has been translated for the
international press archives. It first appeared on 23 June
2036 on Saturn Seydhi (Saturn News), the premium
24-hour Tamil news channel.*

*'A strange epidemic is sweeping across North America
like drop of Brill ink in a glass of water. Many big
cities are under complete government lockdown and
indefinite quarantine. Nevertheless, we have it from
several credible sources that this outbreak is spreading
like wildfire. All nations have been put on a pandemic
red alert. International travel has come to a standstill, as
airports everywhere are shutting down services.*

These two shorts are excerpted from a collection of stories titled
Zombie Da!, slated to be published by Blaft Publications in 2019.

'Breaking News! We have with us the latest government directive: Any members of households that have had friends or relatives visit from the USA in the last one month must report IMMEDIATELY to an emergency virus booth set up by the State Government. Emergency booths are working 24-hours in all major hospitals and clinics across Tamil Nadu. Anyone currently hosting visitors who have been in the USA within the last thirty days is instructed to contact the Government Disease Control hotline 1800-666-6766 immediately.'

Present Day

Translated from a government radio announcement, 19 December 2036:
'Vanakkam, Citizens. The situation today is very much as it has been for the last week: stable. It is too early for the MHCRSTV (Ministry of Highly Contagious Rapid-Spreading Terminal Viruses) to say definitively whether a solution to contain and finally obliterate this virus is close at hand. We do know however that the infected have been contained and neutralized in all major cities across the state. The Government is issuing and will continue to issue combat kits, available at all still-functioning Post Offices, RTO offices, ration shops

and zonal offices. Please ensure that you have inserted the safe biometric chip in your right forearm and in the forearms of dependent family members. Only the Government-certified virus-safe biometric chip will let you access your designated combat kit. Link now.

The Government continues to applaud its living citizens for their vigilance and devotion to civic duty in the face of this darkest chapter in our modern history. We will be disinfected, and never discouraged! Vazhuga Vazhukai! Long Live Life!'

~

Dhanam Catches Some Zs

Dhanam stared at the gang of zombies that had just broken down her front door and messed up her four-colour rangoli. They shuffled in towards her menacingly. There were six of them. The one in front kicked over the terracotta vase she had made in pottery class. It shattered.

This pissed her off.

She put her hair into a tight bun and strode into the kitchen. With the speed of a US commando on a mission, she dragged a stool to the kitchen shelves, stood on it, and from the top-most shelf took down a cane basket filled with empty 25-ml glass bottles bearing 'Goodward's Gripe Water' labels. She whipped three of them out onto the sparkly granite slab of her kitchen counter.

She could hear the undead in the hall moaning, lumbering closer...

Dhanam pulled up a spotless white 10-litre plastic jerrycan from under the kitchen counter, unscrewed the lid, and half-filled three of the Goodward's Gripe Water bottles with kerosene. The liquid was opaque blue, like the Curacao cocktails young things liked to order at resto-bars.

She picked up the cloth used for wiping the counter and tore it into three pieces. She put them into a steel *kinnam*, and judiciously tipped just enough kerosene into the *kinnam* to get the rags moist but not drenched. Then she scrunched each piece into a ball and stuffed it in the mouths of the three Goodward's Gripe Water bottles.

The zombies were now at the arched entrance that opened into the kitchen from the corridor.

She grabbed a box of Cheetah Fight matches off her masala-bottle shelf.

To the fierce beat of a thousand *thavils* playing at Dolby DTS volume in her head, she locked her eyes on them and said '*Vanga da!*' And in one smooth motion, like a hero from a John Woo film, she lit a single matchstick with her right hand, dropped the matchbox, lit the three

Goodward's Gripe Water bottles and hurled them one by one at the first three zombies.

They lit up like *Bhogi* bonfires and dropped onto the vitrified kitchen tiles, writhing.

Drawing on her college-era karate black-belt skills, Dhanam roundhouse-kicked the next in line, popping its head off its neck. It fell like a heavy overripe pumpkin with a wet *thaaawuck* onto the prone form of its burning buddy below.

Only two of them remained. Both were larger, bulkier and oozier than their former team-members. As they weaved towards Dhanam, the zombie on the left lost the bottom half of its jaw mid-step—it fell on the kitchen tiles, scattering teeth like pearls from a broken necklace. Dhanam made her hands into tight fists, angled her body and, shifting her weight for the next strike, started to step back, leading with her dominant right foot...when she slipped on a Hot Wheels toy car and fell backwards heavily, crashing onto the tiles.

She winced. The one with the missing jaw collided with her outstretched feet and toppled onto her. Dhanam was too shocked to scream. Her right hand, which was the only part of her that was zombie-free, desperately searched the bottom shelf within her reach for something to help her out of this predicament.

The zombie on top tried to bite her flailing head,

but it's hard to bite something with half a jaw, and who's going to explain the intricacies of mandibular action to a member of the undead?

Dhanam's hand gained purchase on a rectangular piece of wood. She smiled and yanked it out from the shelf while simultaneously turning on her side through sheer will. The zombie slid sluggishly off her. In the same instance Dhanam brought down what was in her hand and sliced its head off. It was her *aruvamanai*, a family heirloom owned by her great great grandmother. Old, solid iron forged in a small foundry that had once existed in the heart of Kailasapuram. She had always kept its blade katana-sharp: it had sliced and diced onions, snake gourds, yams, mackerel and so much more. But today it was baptized anew as a weapon against the minions spawned from the loins of Hell. Today, it was reborn as a zombie slicer.

Five down and one to go. This last of the standing undead had frozen in its tracks ever since its *dost* had fallen on Dhanam. It now looked at her and moaned. A moan that sounded plaintive, confused, sprinkled with a dash of innocence in its end notes.

Dhanam had no time for analysis. Grabbing her *aruvamanai*, she crouched like an Amazonian jaguar, and in a flash, she leaped—*zuuuuuuuuuuuuuk!* With one mighty slash, she decapitated it, and it fell onto its flaming brothers burning on the floor.

'Everything okay-*va*, Dhanam ma?' yelled Bhaskar Uncle, who lived two floors above Dhanam. He was the head of the of Sunshine Apartments Owner's Association.

'Yes, Uncle!' Dhanam yelled as she stamped out the dying embers, all that was left of the undead.

'Some burning smell is coming, ma…?'

'Uncle, I burned some chapattis. *Avulavu thaan…*'

'Oho, I see, I see. *Yenna* ma, burning something as simple as chapattis? You come learn from Aunty. She will teach you to make A-1 chapatti, phulka, naan, barotta…'

'Okay, Uncle…phone call! Bye!'

Dhanam shut the balcony door and stared at the smouldering heap of undead yuck on her kitchen tiles. She went to her fridge and put six cubes of ice in a tall glass, each cube a tribute to one of the now fully dead zombies who'd had the guts to breach the front door of her home-sweet-home. She then measured out a Patiala peg of Rooh Afza, added the juice of half a lime, and topped it all up with soda. She sat on her dining room chair and swung her legs up on the dining table, took a long sip, and smiled.

~

Kalai Slays the Day

'YEARRRRHH.' A low, hoarse snarl.

Kalai stared at the thing. It looked as if it had sprouted on her amma's terrace garden, its rotting left foot in the *gundu malli* pot and its right in the rose plant with its five yet-to-open rose buds.

It spoke again: 'RAAAWOARRR...'

Kalai lowered her State-Board-syllabus 12th-standard Organic Chemistry textbook (authored by Dr B.S. Tyagi, B.Sc., M.Sc., PhD). It was the size of a standard red construction brick, and had expertly soft-stitched binding. Number of pages: 450. A textbook that clearly meant business.

The Foulness took two heavy steps forward.

PHATCHURRK! PHATCHURRK! The innocent flowerpots shattered.

It grinned at Kalai in the same *mokkai* way that opposite-house Karthik (first-year B.Com) grinned whenever he saw her.

The zombie stretched out its arms, as if playing *kannam-boochi* with Kalai, but cheating, playing with its eyes wide open.

Kalai did a quick 180-degree scan of her immediate surroundings. To her left was a broken mosquito bat lying on the floor. She bent down and picked it up. In her other hand, she flipped over her Organic Chemistry textbook, holding it by its thick spine.

The thing lunged!

With the lightning fast precision of a 10th Dan, Kalai brought the mosquito bat and Organic Chemistry textbook together in a fatal clap!

PACHAAAAAAAAAAAAAAAK!!!

A disgusting *kanji* of putrid blood and rotted brains exploded over her and onto the terrace floor. The headless abomination fell over like an overstuffed bundle of freshly ironed clothes falling off a TVS 50 moped.

As Kalai wiped her face on her sleeve, she locked eyes with Karthik, who was standing with his mouth wide open on the opposite terrace.

'Matches *irruka?*' she asked aloud.

Karthik shut his mouth and nodded weakly.

Kalai carefully put down her Organic Chemistry textbook. She gestured to him with her right hand, in an action that clearly denoted she was asking him to throw her the box of matches.

Karthik, as if under hypnosis, put his right hand in his track pants pocket. Today, said track pants were matched with a body-hugging T-shirt that said 'YOLO!!' under a graphic of Che Guevara's face.

Karthik threw Kalai the matches. She caught them deftly in her left hand. She lit eight matchsticks in one strike and dropped the large flame on what remained of the Unnatural Thing at her feet. It blazed like a bonfire in a K-Jo shot-in-Switzerland duet song.

Kalai's face glowed like raw honey in its light. She looked at Karthik and smiled.

'Coming to eat bhelpuri?' she asked coolly. 'Bhelpuri *saapada variya?*'

OMNI8

Vinayak Varma

'On our NH66,
There's nothing left to fix,
Coz the land's been greened,
And our airs are clean!
Yeah, we've hit this for a six!
Huzzah!'

National Highway 66 smashed through the Marana terrain like an angry obsidian fist. Mirages radiated off it in fat waves, primed to melt unprepped tyres and shoe-soles into rubber puddles. The wind squealed as it raked through the breaks and cracks in the burning gravel. Bala the pilot shuddered and tightened his cross-straps.

His passengers, the envoys, had enjoyed the previous leg of their journey, down the new Halethara ghat road leading to the Highway. That road had been nice and flat, easy on the spine, and well shaded by the Arb. The delegation had lounged around the cabin the whole time, sharing a gourd of gooseberry wine and telling each other jokes and stories of their youth.

Now they stowed away the wine and secured themselves using belts and bootleashes to keep from bouncing off the carriage and onto the road. Their cargo, an ovoid blue-green storage pod, had already been tethered to the deck with gravity bands. NH66 would be far less forgiving, they knew, with its dustwinds, its surface like pitted teeth, and its hunger for living flesh.

The surroundings, too, had considerably worsened. It was immediately apparent where the panchayat's limits ended and Marana district began. While the panchayat was in a fully updated Grade 3 district, the Marana was a long wedge of archaic horror where the government's mimetech had failed to calm the ravages of the Dim.

To the west of the carriage, between the Highway and the acid sea, there lay a great, lifeless marsh shrouded in plastic waste, the bones of birds and sea creatures, and broken, rotting palm trees that tore through the slime like claws. Thousands of giant concrete tetrapods formed battle-lines across the shore, their ranks broken every few kilometres by dunes of oil-blackened sand.

To the east was a flat, semi-industrial landscape, pinned down by a railway track that started and ended nowhere. The track was flanked by colonial rail bungalows, grain silos, assembly yards, sludge-grey housing development colonies that were once painted pink, purple and neon green, and rows of asbestos shanties falling into one another—all long-abandoned.

Further up the road were mounds and mounds of rusty goods cars, charcoal-grey fields that had shimmered with ragi, honge and kodo in the pre-Dim days, acres of gorse and zombie cactus, and ashen shells of factories and crematoria that lay about in heaps like wounded dragons. From the far horizon, a litter of mined-down, hollowed-out hills sneered at the carriage as it hobbled down the highway.

There were no Arbing machines or smartspores in this district, nor any Payengites, for even such miracles had their limits. What the eyes saw here could batter the heart and depress the mind, peel away the new-found optimism that had so rejuvenated the gram-panchayats and civic centres of Swarajia. And so the envoys quickly donned their shadegogs and blindfolds and stared down at their feet, avoiding the windows and each other, resigned to silently brooding the rest of the way. Only Bala still watched the road, and even he tried to squint away the scenery and sing the old Highway Anthem to offset his dread of Marana.

> *'On our NH66, they say,*
> *We may ever keep our fears at bay.*
> *It's all peace and joy*
> *For every girl and boy*
> *On our happy, happy highway!'*

The song made little sense post-Dim, but the more superstitious Swarajians still believed it was a good ward against the Highway's ill-temper. Bala had already sung it a few dozen times since the carriage alighted NH66, in several genres and time-signatures of his own devising, before the dustwinds finally thinned and the road got smoother, and he noticed little bursts of green dotting the shoreline. Adbursts for restaurants and motels started beaming onto his gogs, fuzzy at first, but increasingly crisp and insistent as he drove on. And finally, a colossal horned-silhouette loomed up from the horizon, fast-growing, blocking out the sun and sky entirely.

'At long last,' Bala muttered. 'May their holy Gau raksh us all.'

He reached down below his chair and yanked at a string that ran from the cockpit to a bell inside the passenger cabin. It rang thrice, and the envoys hurriedly sat up and undid their facewear so they could peer outside. Bala stuck his head through the window and yelled, for good measure, 'Gau ahead! Gau ahead! Yuvabase One, aunties and uncles! We're in Dharma district, ketto!'

'At long last,' the envoys muttered. 'May their holy Gau raksh us all.'

Bala cranked the engine and sped onwards. Within minutes, the air had cleared completely, and the Gau stood revealed in all her divine glory.

Every known shastra had been employed in the construction of this First Yuvabase Civic Centre. The city was max-mimeteched to receive continuous Arb updates, and its skyscrapers had all been arrayed into a complex system of staggered heights and distances. It had been designed this way for a three-fold purpose that was simultaneously utilitarian and spiritual: to allow every green surface equal access to the sunstream, to optimally project prayer vibrations into the cosmos above, and for the buildings to collectively form the shape of a gigantic silver cow. Bursting with pride for having built a monument so large and shiny that it was even visible from the Moon, the first residents of the city had named themselves the Guardians of the Atom and the Universe, or GAUs.

The carriage approached the city portal, under a long udder-shaped shadow, and passed into one of the active scanner-arches. The projection wall by the driver's side lit up and displayed a gif of a fat milkman smiling and bowing with folded hands.

'May the great and holy Gau raksh us all,' said the sentry scanbot. 'I repeat: may the great and holy Gau raksh us all. Please speak your assigned VPR phrase when the screen turns blue.'

'May the great and holy Gau raksh us all,' said Bala, as directed.

'You are most welcome at YCC1, GAU City, seat of clean thought and good habit, gift and joy for all who thrive under the benevolent eye of our divine Gau. All inquiries are pending. Are you the representative or travel agent for all members in your group?'

'Yes,' said Bala.

'Authorization required for body-scans of all Swarajian human passengers present.'

'Granted.'

'Scanning and cross-checking with national citizen records. Kindly confirm the following details. Passenger count: five humans travelling from Halepura, Nila panchayat, Malabar district.'

'Yes.'

'Four Halevasis in the seventh cent-quadrant, oldmax.'

One of the envoys harrumphed from the back, annoyed at the affront.

'Yes,' said Bala. 'Designated envoys of Nila, conveying the voice of our respected Moopan Razia Begum.'

'Noted. Names and residences: Mary P., 2B; Purushottaman S., 4B; Queenavati L., 9K; and Senthil M., 4F. Approximate ages: 174 years, 155 years, 153 years, and 150 years, respectively.'

'That is correct,' said Bala, pointing to the cabin behind him.

'Noted. One Halevasi, vehicle pilot, in the fifth cent-quadrant, oldmid. Name and residence: Bala M., 3K. Approximate age: 112 years.'

'Yes,' said Bala. 'I am he.'

'Noted. Med report: two cases of advanced cell-breakdown, both contained within med-prescribed limits. No evidence of pre-mimetech diseases in any passenger; healthmax. Kindly confirm.'

'You are correct,' said Bala.

'You have duly qualified for a category upgrade. Congratulations! You are now eligible for free parking in all Corporation lots. Jai Gau.'

'Jai Gau.'

'Scanning for Ajna implants. No A-ID tags. No genemods. No lung-tats. No subdermal records.'

'Correct.'

'Are you first-gen BioSign users?'

'No.'

'Are you Janapriya Party subscribers?'

'No.'

'Are you surveillance-agnostics? Kindly confirm.'

'Yes. That is correct.'

'Noted. Entry points duly deducted. Parking access revoked. Temple and Mutra Lake access limited. Processing data. Kindly wait.'

'Okay.'

'Scanning transport and cargo,' said the scanbot. 'One Mooshika EL-fifty-eight Perambulator Carriage.'

'Yes.'

'Noted. Scanning. Six F&B bags, and five luggage boxes containing personal clothing, toiletries, meds and ent-consoles.'

'Yes.'

'Scanning. One unidentified object. Unable to verify.'

'Ah. O Holy Scanner, sir,' said Bala, gabbling booktongue in his nervousness, 'that to which you make kind reference is the vessel we humbly transport. Our esteemed cargo.'

'What are the contents of said cargo?'

'Sincerely, we do not know.'

'Are you not its owners?'

'We are not, nil. We have not ascertained the vessel's provenance. It is sans owner, sender, purpose, within our ken. However, it is max lightweight, and when touched by human skin, it produces a wild whistling. We believe it must belong to Yuvabase members. Hence, we request city access. And we request an appointment with the corporator of your most holy civic centre, so as to present his guardianship with this humble gift.'

'Your requests are under temporary suspension. Kindly identify the contents and origin of your cargo. Verbal acknowledgement required. You have three attempts remaining.'

'We do not know, I say again,' said Bala. 'We were unable to prise it open. Two weeks prior, it made rapid descent from the sky, borne by a slender parachute, sans markings. We do not know whence it was thus propelled. We believe it was intended for your masters, since our own sector does not presently possess the capability for non-terrestrial broadcasts or boon-requests of any manner.'

'Unable to process event transcript. Unable to verify.'

'Why do you not perhaps scan the object? I shall remove it from the carriage, for your kind pleasure.'

'Your request is denied,' said the scanbot. 'Kindly identify the contents and origin of your cargo. Verbal acknowledgement required. You have one attempt remaining.'

'You do not seem to understand, sir. We know not what it is, I repeat. We are unable to gaze within. Your advanced scanners should be able to map it, Gau willing.'

'Attempt to engage scanner denied. Potential terror threat identified.'

'What? How have you concluded thus?'

'Potential incendiary device detected.'

'No, no,' said Bala, alarmed. 'You misinterpret me, sir. Let us begin again, this holy scanning process…'

'Potential attempt to trigger device using scan beam,' said the scanbot. 'Event detected and record duly relayed to Suraksha services. Kindly park your vehicle and present yourselves at seva window D, to your left.'

'Allay this security event, sir, O Scanner. It matters not. We wish not to cause such a fright to your good selves. We shall leave as we have arrived. I thus cancel our access request. We thank you for expending your valuable time on our account.'

'Kindly confirm cancellation of city-access request.'

'It is confirmed.'

'Noted. Request duly cancelled. Temporary entry application deleted. Please be on your way. May the great and holy Gau raksh and kshamik you.'

'May the great Gau raksh us all,' Bala responded, and turned the carriage around.

The cockpit intercom beeped and crackled alive. 'What's the matter?' asked Mary, from the cabin. 'Why aren't we going in?'

'They didn't let us through,' Bala said into his

microphone. 'They think we're carrying a bomb. If I'd waited any longer, we'd have been arrested.'

'Crap. So what do we do now? We head back to Nila?'

'The Moopan won't let us hear the end of it. I doubt if she'll even let us back in. Not with that damn pod still on us. So, no. Let's try our luck at YCC2. I'm told those folks enjoy a bitta bit-music.'

'Okay, okay. Good. Lettus. Forthwith.'

'For the record, I hate lying to govbots like this,' said Bala. 'This mission is going to wreck our citizen ratings, you know.'

'Consider the alternative,' said Mary. 'The relentless good cheer. The singing and the headaches. Not to mention Razia's poor temper. I'm too old for all that.'

'Hmm.'

'Having to live with that creature is a fate far worse than rating-deficits or the stress of lying.'

'I guess you're right. Let the Yuvabases deal with it. Gau knows they have the energy for it.'

'So let's go. Are we getting back on NH66?'

'I'm afraid so. We'll have to double back for a few kilometres until we can turn off at the bypass.'

'Okay. We'll strap back in. Carry on.'

The best as well as the worst thing about driving on NH66, Bala reflected, was the singular lack of insects flying into his windshield. It kept his carriage bright and clean, but it also slammed home the pervasiveness of mortality in the Dim zones. Every minute spent here felt like a slight acceleration in cell-loss.

The bypass road to Shoonya City, though off the Highway, was still in Marana, and prone to some of the district's worst dysfunctions. While the Highway was merely hard on the senses, the bypass was also a breeding ground for a host of pre-Arb bioparticles. Once breathed in, they could fill the brain with maddening echoes from ancient ent-media, or infect the nerves with jerky-limb, or even induce a coma. Shoonyans rarely visited their Gau City cousins, or vice versa, for these very fears.

'Up your window glass, stow your devices and get your oxies on,' Bala said into the microphone. 'Bypass ahead.'

'I shall inform the others,' Mary responded.

Bala put the engine into high gear, and the carriage hurtled towards the bypass. As he steered past the toll booths and through the gates, he pulled his own oxygen mask out of the dash and wrapped it across his face.

'Close call,' he muttered to himself, as an ochre cloud descended on the carriage, soaking its every outer inch in bioparticle.

> 'Our NH66 is best!
> It aces every quality test!

It's so smooth and flat,
Like a yoga mat!
You can even lie on it and rest!

'Our NH66 is bzzzzt...
It makes our bzzzt-dankanakana-
-dankanakana dankanakana-
bzzzt -hoyya hoyya hoyya ho-
-hoyya hoyya hoyya- bzzzt...'

Bala looked around the cockpit in panic. The windows were up all the way. The windshield had no cracks in it. The evac-chute was also sealed. From where could the pollen have entered?

'Bzzzt -makanakago-
makanakago- bzzzt...'

He stopped the carriage and switched on the servicebot.

'Servicer, please scan for—*dankanakana-dankanakana*—blast it! Scan for influx of bio-active entparticulates, radiopollen category, archmax.'

A vehicle schematic popped up on the display. One end of it blinked yellow.

'Passenger cabin, rear window,' the servicebot said.

Bala looked under his seat and saw fine tendrils of

ochre mist forking out of the comms pipe connecting the two compartments. He immediately rang the cabin bell and shouted into the microphone.

'Hello? Uncles! Aunties! Can anyone hear me?'

'I am—*chayya chayya chayya*—cannot make the—*kukukukukuku*—here,' said a faint voice.

'Chenthil maama, is that you?' asked Bala.

'Yes,' said Senthil.

'Rear—*hoyya ho*—dammit! Your rear window! It's not fully shut! Bioparticles are—*marugo-marugo-jorugo-jorugo*—ARGH! Shut the rear window, uncle!'

'I see it,' said Senthil. 'Hold—*hai hukku hai hukku*—hold on!'

Bala looked down at the servicer display anxiously, waiting for the highlighted section to turn grey. A few more minutes of exposure would unhinge them all.

'Chenthil maama,' said Bala, 'please confirm—*chikku bukku chikku bukku*—shit! Chenthil maama!'

'I've—*chooey mooey chooey mooey*—can whoosh now! The window's shut! Do it!'

'Servicer, begin ventscrub,' said Bala. 'Whoo—*ammapete ayyampete thenampete*—dammit! Servicer! Begin ventscrub! Whooshie level five!'

The carriage shook and wheezed as the cleaner and air conditioner worked in tandem to blast all lingering allergens out of the two compartments.

'Chenthil maama,' said Bala, when the whooshing was done. 'Are you okay?'

'Yes,' said Chenthil. 'But barely. I'm still hearing things.'

'The others?'

'Puru is fine.'

'Good.'

'Queenie's mumbling "*rumbumbum-aarumbum*" over and over.'

'Shit.'

'It'll wear off soon, hopefully. As for Mary…well.'

'What's wrong with Mary auntie?'

'She's unconscious. Very shallow breathing. The particles may have entered her bloodstream.'

'Oh no. Have you checked her eyes?'

'Yes. Sclera turning yellow already.'

'Chenthil maama?' said Bala.

'Yes?'

'Shoonya is almost four hours away. And the hospitals there won't take us in without security clearance. What if things pan out the same way it did at the Gau?'

'It's possible.'

'The risk is too high. Auntie won't make it.'

'She won't make it if we head back to the Gau either. They're not going to let us in now if they didn't then.'

'I'm going to turn us back around anyway,' said Bala.

'And…?'

'We'll be off the bypass in a few minutes. I'll make a rest stop on NH66 as soon as I find some shade.'

'To what end?'

Bala put the engine into gear.

'We're going to open the pod and let Omni8 do its thing.'

'Bala, our entire mission is to get rid of that thing.'

'How else do we save Mary auntie? She's got radiopollen in the brain. She'll be lost for good unless we do something quickly.'

'Terrible idea, Bala.'

'This entire trip was a terrible idea. We should've thrown the damn thing in the firepit when we had the chance.'

'You're questioning our Moopan's wisdom?'

'I'm questioning her sense of humour. It would've been funny to watch one of the Yuvabases go bleezoid for a few days, sure, but at such a cost? That's mental!'

'You go too far, Bala.'

'Let's save this debate for the next Panchayat meeting,' said Bala, and twisted the navstick.

The carriage spun around to face the toll gates.

> *'NH66, so fine!*
> *NH66, your mine!*

You make my knees go weak!
Your gravel game's on fleek!
I've hearted you since '29!'

They trundled to a halt next to an old electroport junction, a few kilometres down the Highway. The charger boxes and solar arrays at the junction's parking zone had been knocked down and stencilled over by artsters, and every panel bore the same symbol of the end-times: a flamingo with blackened feathers. The main station building had partially caved in, and the roots of a dead banyan poured out of the hole like knotted hair.

'We shouldn't be here. This place is peak Dim,' said Senthil.

'At least the air's relatively cleaner,' said Bala.

'Really?' said Senthil. 'It reeks of chemic and rot.'

'No particulates, though.'

Purushottaman and Queenavati carried Mary's inert body out of the passenger cabin and laid her down in the building's shaded portico. Bala and Senthil unbanded the storage pod and placed it on the curb outside, so it could catch some sunstream and anim-up.

'How do we do this?' asked Bala. 'I'm not familiar with its activation protocols.'

'I'll do it,' said Queenavati.

She squatted and placed both her palms against the pod's eggshell surface.

'Helloooo! If there's something in there, we need you to come out now!' she said.

She stared at the pod expectantly. Nothing happened.

'There must be more to it than that, surely,' said Bala.

'This is what the Moopan did after the pod landed. I was there, I saw it happen. It worked then,' said Queenavati.

'Try again, Auntie,' said Bala. 'Maybe it didn't hear you properly.'

She leaned in again. Before she could repeat her command, the pod began to quiver and rumble.

'Delayed response,' said Queenavati, and stood back up with a grunt.

The pod emitted a long, shrill beep. Pink dots appeared on its surface, running together and forming a message: a line of Hanzi, followed by a gif of a cat playing a keymonica.

'I think it's in Huayu,' said Queenavati. 'I don't know the script. Puru, can you translate this?'

'I can,' said Purushottaman. 'Let me see. It says…Ah… Okay, got it. It reads: "Say hello to activate Omni8 in your chosen language." Looks like you got the order of events wrong, Queenie. This is where you say hello.'

'Oh, alright. HELLOOOOOO!' said Queenavati.

The pod beeped again and cracked into two neat

hemi-ellipsoids. Something splashed onto the hot concrete, dissipated briefly, then regrouped and slowly swarmed into the air above the pod, twinkling and buzzing as it arose, eventually shaping itself into a translucent gold spectre.

'HELLO, HELLO, HELLO!' it said.

'Hello,' repeated Queenavati.

There was a low whistle, followed by a cheerful chiptune melody.

'HELLO, HELLO AND HELLO AGAIN!' sang the spectre. 'I am, I am Omni8! I'm your friend! I'm your future! I am so full of every feature! I am Omni-everything! Pa-pa-pa-pa-pa-pa, hey!'

'Oh Gau,' said Senthil through gritted teeth. 'Here we go again.'

'I am, I am, I am all! I see all! I do all! I go anywhere at all! I'm so glad! I'm so bright! I can make your...'

'Hi! Sorry to interrupt your lovely song, Omni8,' said Bala. 'We need your help rather urgently.'

'Yes, I can help!' sang Omni8. 'I can, because I am Omni8! I don't, I don't discriminate! You may have feet or you may have hooves! Yo, I'm the tech with all the moves! Pa-pa-pa-pa...'

'Okay, yes, thanks,' said Bala, 'but we really don't have time for this. Look there,' he said, pointing at Mary. 'Our friend has been contaminated with bioparticles. We need you to disinfect and revive her.'

'I can fix what's troubling! I am Omni-everything!' sang Omni8. 'I can, I can heal the sick! Will do, will do, double-quick! Please say yes to confirm.'

'Yes, yes, yes!' said Bala. 'Do it!'

'OKAY! OKAY! OKAY!' sang Omni8. 'I'm on it like a comet! I'll grill 'em and I'll kill 'em!'

The chiptune subsided into a light susurration. The Omni8 swarm fluttered over to Mary, turning emerald as it moved. It spread out and gently cocooned her body.

'I hope this works,' said Senthil. 'I hope it's worth it.'

'Please relax, Chenthil maama,' said Bala.

'The ailment is identified, oh yay yay yay!' said Omni8. 'Clearing contaminants in under two minutes and thirty seconds. Yip! Yip! Yip!'

'Isn't that nice,' said Purushottaman, who had been visiting his brother in the next village when the Moopan first unlocked the pod. 'It's being so positive.'

'So positive, yes,' said Senthil, scowling, remembering only too well the loud, sleepless nights following Omni8's release, and the seemingly impossible task of getting it back into the pod.

'One minute and fifteen seconds,' said Omni8. 'Almost there, hey hey hey! Almost—oh ho ho! I'm pre-deadline! I'm a diamond mine! I'm such a trooper! I'm so super!'

'Can any of you understand what it's saying?' asked

Bala. The other envoys shook their heads. 'Sounds like archspeak.'

There was a muffled moan from the cocoon, and the emerald swarm bubbled out and swept away from Mary. She immediately sat up, yawning and rubbing her eyes. The Halevasis rushed to her, cheering and clapping in their relief.

'We thought we'd lost you!' said Queenavati.

'A miracle!' said Purushottaman.

'*Bzzt-gemini-gemini-gemini-gemini-gavani-gavani-* what?' said Mary.

'Oh no,' said Bala. 'I don't think she's out of it yet.'

'They're echoes,' said Queenavati. 'Recalcitrant N-patterns. Don't worry. They'll dissipate with time and care.'

Senthil pointed at Omni8, which was back outside, turning golden again in the sunstream. 'What do we do with that thing?' he asked. 'We can't take it home with us. We'll all go mad.'

'But why?' asked Purushottaman. 'I no longer understand all the fuss. Omni8 seems perfectly useful.'

'It is and it isn't,' said Bala.

'Useful, useful Omni8!' sang Omni8, hearing its name mentioned. 'Perfect, perfect Omni8! I'm your mate! I'm your fate! One and only Omni8! Yay!'

It floated over to Purushottaman and attempted to hug him.

'I'm your heart! I'm your friend!' sang Omni8. 'I'm your start, and I'm your end!'

Purushottaman attempted to struggle free, but Omni8 gripped him harder. Senthil bent over in laughter.

'I take it back!' said Purushottaman. 'Help me!'

Omni8 unfurled and bowed. 'Yes, I can help!' it sang. 'I can, because I am Omni8! I don't, I don't discriminate! Pa-pa-pa-pa-pa!'

'Help me, Omni8,' said Bala, stepping forward.

'Omni8 can help, oh yes!' it sang. 'I can clean up every mess!'

'Great idea,' said Bala. 'I need you to clean up the Highway. Clean it up and restore its health. Bring back the natural balance. Can you do that?'

'Yes, I can! I can try! I shall clean e'en if I fry! Please say yes to confirm!'

'Yes! Yes!'

'Good thinking,' said Queenavati. 'That should buy us a few years of peace.'

'A futile endeavour, indeed,' said Senthil, approvingly. 'Nothing can save NH66, not even this thing.'

'I am, I am, I am all! I see all! I do all! I go anywhere at all! 100 percent sunstrength required for Dim-zone rejuvenation. Sunstrength at 12 percent. Omni8 will sing while you wait! Omni8 will entertain! Omni8 will ease your pain! Pa-pa-pa-pa-pa...'

'Crap,' said Queenavati. 'It's trying to keep us engaged. What now?'

'Omni8, can you bring me some chocolate to eat while I wait?' asked Bala.

'I am, I am Omni8!' sang Omni8. 'I can bring you chocolate! It's rarer than rare, but Omni8 knows where! Scanning infoband A...Scanning infoband B...Ho-ho-ho! Hey-hey-hey! 300 grams of chocolate found at ultramart #XI, geo-sector Euro.'

'You're a genius, Bala,' said Queenavati.

'May I procure this for you?' asked Omni8. 'Say yes to confirm.'

'Yes,' said Bala. 'Do it!'

'OKAY!' said Omni8. 'I'm going like a Boeing! I'll catch it and I'll hatch it!'

'What is it saying? What's a bow-ing?' asked Purushottaman.

'No clue,' said Senthil.

'Yip! Yip! Yip!' sang Omni8. 'Your task will be achieved in under sixteen hours and twenty-seven minutes. Kindly wait here.'

With that, it vanished.

'Shall we leave?' asked Bala.

'Yes,' said Senthil. 'The damn thing's good with deadlines. Let's go.'

'You're an—*eyy-ji-ohh-ji-loh-ji-suno-ji*—Bala,' said Mary.

The envoys climbed into the carriage and sped off down the NH66, rushing to beat the last light.

> 'NH66, my friend,
> I know your every dip and bend!
> I'm astounded
> At the way you keep me grounded!
> Stay with me till the bitter end,
> O NH66, my friend!'

At noon the next day, a hard, hot dustwind blew across the Highway. It blew past the vacant rail bungalows and silos and shanties, over the burnt fields and the crumbling factories, screaming as it rushed through the cracks in the asphalt. At last the wind reached an old electroport junction, where it paused long enough to eject a swarm of silver particles. The particles spun around, collected into a pool, and expanded to form a shimmering spectre that hung in the air like a broken promise.

'I am, I am Omni8!' it wailed. 'I've failed to bring you chocolate! Euro is a scary place, an absolute disgrace! Their war-tech really hates the East! They're really, really well-policed! I couldn't even enter! They nearly lasered-out my centre! Pa-pa-pa-pa-pa-pa-pa...! Hello?'

No one responded, and so it grew more agitated.

'Omni8 won't fail you twice!' it sang. 'I'm a quality

device! Scanning for pending tasks. "Clean up and restore the Highway." Checking all systems. 100 percent sunstrength required for Dim-zone rejuvenation. Sunstrength at 100 percent. Yip! Yip! Yip! Yip! Hey hey!'

Omni8 extended a tentacle into the ground beneath it and began to churn the earth. It sifted and reshaped the matter, molecule by molecule, twisting this and splitting that. When it was done, a section of the earth had turned from grey to brown, and a tiny shoot of bamboo had sprung through.

'Oh yay yay yay yay yay!' sang Omni8. 'Ho ho ho! Hey hey hey! Gonna cask this task! Gonna dish this wish! Gonna fix your NH66!'

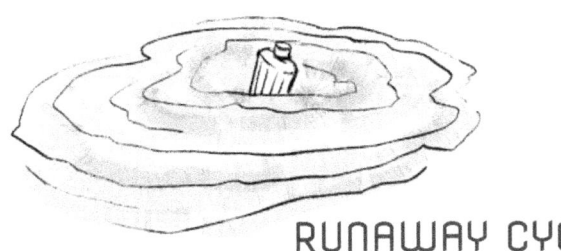

RUNAWAY CYCLONE

(THE STORY OF THE MISSING ONE)

J.C. Bose /
Translated by Bodhisattva Chattopadhyay

Part I: A Scientific Mystery

A few years ago, a supernatural event was observed. It had rocked the scientific communities of America and Europe. A number of articles were published in various scientific journals to explain the phenomenon. But until now no explanation for the event has been found satisfactory.

On 28 September Calcutta's leading English daily[*] published the following news they received from Shimla:

This translation of 'Runaway Cyclone' / 'The Story of The Missing One' was previously published in *Strange Horizons*.

[*] 1896: *Englishman.*

Shimla Meteorological Office, 27 September: A cyclone in the Bay of Bengal is imminent.[*]

On 29 September the aforementioned daily published the following news: *Meteorological Office, Alipore: A tremendous cyclone is about to strike Bengal in two days. A danger signal has been put up on Diamond Harbour.*

On the 30th, the news was extremely frightening: *The Barometer fell by two inches in the last half hour. By ten o'clock tomorrow Calcutta will face the worst and most dangerous cyclone in years.*[†]

No one slept that night in Calcutta. The timorous souls stayed awake in fear of their uncertain future.

On 1 October the sky remained cloudy, and a few drops of rain fell during the day. It remained dark throughout the day, but at about four in the evening the

---

[*] Cyclones have been common phenomena in Bengal. There were four major cyclones in the Bay of Bengal in the nineteenth century alone. Of these, a particularly destructive one had been the great Calcutta cyclone of 1864 in which over 50,000 lives were lost. According to the *Encyclopaedia of Hurricanes, Typhoons and Cyclones* (David Longshore, New York: Facts on File, Inc., 2008, p. 257-58), the Meteorological Department in Kolkata was established by the British East India Company after this cyclone.

[†] At this point a number of lines of the 1896 version have been left out, most significantly the line reported by the Reuters agent to the *Times*: 'The Capital of our Indian Empire is in danger.' By the time the story was republished with the new title, Calcutta was no longer the capital city.

sky suddenly became clear. There was no trace of the cyclone.

The next day the Meteorological Department sent the following news to the newspaper office: *The cyclone that was to strike Calcutta has left the Bay of Bengal and has probably gone off in another direction in the Indian Ocean.*

However, despite the attempts made by many scientists to follow the cyclone's trails, the cyclone's new direction could not be discovered.

Then the same English daily* published the following news: *Now it is certain that scientific knowledge is completely false.*

Another daily† published the following: *If science is false then why should the taxpayers be burdened by the totally unreliable Meteorological department?*

Various other dailies‡ joined as chorus: *Let it go! Scrap it!*

The government was in a fix. A few days ago new equipment worth over a lakh had been purchased for the Meteorological Department. Now those items would not even sell for the price of broken glass bottles. Besides, where would one transfer the Chief Officer of the Meteorological Department?

---

* 1896: *Englishman.*

† 1896: *Daily News.*

‡ 1896: *Pioneer, Civil and Military Gazette, Statesman.*

In dire straits the government appealed to the Calcutta Medical College: 'We wish to appoint a new Chair at the Medical College. Lectures would be delivered on the following topic: "On the Effect of Variation of Barometric Pressure on the Human System." The principal of the Medical College wrote back:

A wonderful suggestion. A decrease in air pressure enhances blood circulation in the human body. This would undoubtedly help rejuvenate the body. However, the citizens of Calcutta are under the following pressures at the moment:

1st, Air. Pressure per square inch: 15 pounds.

2nd, Malaria. Pressure per square inch: 20 pounds.

3rd, Patented medicines. Pressure per square inch: 30 pounds.

4th, University. Pressure per square inch: 50 pounds.

5th, Income tax. Pressure per square inch: 80 pounds.

6th, Municipal tax. Pressure per square inch: 1 tonne.

The relief of a few inches of air pressure would be like removing a handful of twigs from an already heavy load. Thus starting this Chair in Calcutta might not have particularly beneficial or noticeable effects on the residents of this city. In the hills of Shimla the air pressure as well as other pressures are comparatively lesser. Hence it would be better if the said Chair was appointed at Shimla because the effects would be more noticeable there.

The government remained silent on the issue after this. The Meteorological Department managed to survive this particular crisis.

The issue of the cyclone however remained unresolved.

A scientist published an article in Nature. His theory was that the cyclone was dispersed by the gravitational pull of an invisible comet. These are all mere speculations.

Even now the issue raises cycloney debates in the scientific community. At the British Association convention at Oxford, a German professor presented an erudite paper on the 'runaway cyclone' phenomenon, which astounded his peers.* According to the Professor, 'A cyclone is merely a form of the atmosphere. Let us first examine how the atmosphere came into being. When the Earth was simply molten metallic matter that had come out of the sun, it did not have an atmosphere. How oxygen, nitrogen and hydrogen came together out of this molten matter is still one of the mysteries of creation. Even more mysterious and fascinating is the evolution of life. Let us assume that the atmosphere somehow came into being.

---

* 1896: Herr Stürm F. R. S., 'On a Vanished Cyclone.' While the 1896 version contains the title, the long extract from the Professor's paper/speech is not a part of it.

The greater problem is why this atmosphere does not dissolve and vanish into space. This is because of Earth's gravitational pull. Gravity works according to relative mass. That which is heavier is subject to more gravitational force and is therefore relatively tied to its own position on the earth. The lighter object is less influenced by gravity and is therefore relatively free. This is why when we mix oil and water, oil—which is lighter—generally floats to the surface. Hydrogen, being lighter, tries to escape the Earth's atmosphere—but it is not completely free of the gravitational pull. However, we doubt if the truth of relative mass is applicable to areas other than physics. For instance, in the country called India, the men are heavy and relatively free while, the women, who are comparatively light, are tied to the domestic space. In any case, only matter remains attached to the Earth by virtue of its gravity. After the death of matter it is free of the Earth. When man gives up his ghost, the force of gravity no longer restricts his movement. Some people say that even in death man is not free of Earth, because even ghosts have to move under the commands of the Theosophical society. In the case of matter, however, it is incorrect to say that it attains five states—because we see only three. When bombarded with radium, matter breaks down into three states: alpha, beta, and gamma. Thus when matter is broken down, the non-matter escapes into an unknown space. While living, however, it is impossible to escape the force of gravity.'

While the professor did provide a scientific explanation for why matter does not escape into space, he failed to point out why the cyclone suddenly disappeared in the Bay of Bengal.

The truth of the matter is known to only one person in this world—me. In the next part I will give a detailed explanation of the phenomenon.

Part II

I fell extremely ill some years ago. I was in bed for almost a month. The doctor said that a sea journey was absolutely necessary; without it I would not survive another spell of the illness. So I decided to go to Ceylon.

The illness had taken its toll on my once abundant hair. One day my eight-year-old daughter came up to me and asked: 'Daddy, what is an island?' Before I could answer she took hold of the few locks of hair left on my otherwise smooth head and said: 'Here are the islands.' After a while she said: 'I have put a bottle of "Kuntal Keshari" in your bag. Use it every day during your journey; otherwise in the salty sea-water even these few islands will vanish.'

The story of how 'Kuntal Keshari' was invented is very interesting. A British Sahib came to India with his circus troupe. The star attraction of the circus was a lion with a huge and lustrous black mane. By a stroke of misfortune the lion lost its thick hair during the voyage to India because of a microbial disease. When the ship landed, one could not see much difference between the lion and a hairless street dog. The helpless circus manager prostrated himself before a sanyasi, touched his feet, and with folded hands asked for a solution. A Christian, and an Englishman at that! The sanyasi was impressed with the man's devotion and as blessing gave him a bottle of oil whose formulae had come to the sanyasi in a dream. This is the same oil that later became famous as 'Kuntal Keshari'. Applying this oil helped the lion get its mane back within a week. For all bald men and their partners this oil holds a special fascination. This news was published for the public good in all newspapers of the country. A leading monthly magazine even featured the news on its cover.

On 28 September, I set sail on the *Chusan*. The first two days were uneventful and pleasant. On the 1st, however, the sea assumed a strange and hostile form and the sea-breeze stopped completely. Even the surface of the sea remained taut. We were all struck by the sad look on the Captain's face. He told us that very soon an extremely violent cyclone was going to crash upon us. Being far from the coast, our future was now in God's hands.

Soon thereafter the sky became overcast with thick

black clouds. It became dark almost instantly and some strong winds from afar came and struck our ship several times. I have only a faint idea of what happened thereafter. All of a sudden it was as if the angry giants of yore had returned and come to destroy the earth. The sounds of the cyclone winds mixed with the sounds of the angry sea and made the music of destruction all around us. Waves upon waves hit our boat and rocked it from all sides. A huge wave took away our mast and lifeboat with it. Our last day was upon us.

One remembers one's loved ones when his final moments are near. I remembered my loved ones, and strangely, even my daughter's joke about my sparse hair:

'Daddy, I have put a bottle of "Kuntal Keshari" in your bag.'

Suddenly I remembered what I had read recently in a scientific journal about the effects of oil on waves. I remembered that oil calms the surface of moving water. I took out my bottle of 'Kuntal Keshari' that very moment from my bag and with great difficulty climbed up to the deck. I saw that a gigantic mountain-like wave was coming to strike us down.

I abandoned all hope, opened the cap of the 'Kuntal Keshari' bottle and threw it at the sea. Like magic the sea became calm, and the wonderful cooling oil even calmed the entire atmosphere. The sun came up in a second.

Thus we were spared from a certain death and it is for this reason the cyclone never reached Calcutta. How many thousands were saved from an untimely death simply by this one bottle of hair oil, who can say?

Translator's Note

This story by J.C. Bose (1858–1937) is regarded as one of the first works of early science fiction in Bengali, and one of the first science-fiction stories in India. It was first published in 1896 as 'Niruddesher Kahini' ('The Story of the Missing One'), the winning entry in the Kuntalin Story Competition. Kuntalin was a popular hair oil back then. The inventor and owner of the oil, Hemendramohan Basu, instituted a promotional annual fiction competition from 1896 onwards, with the precondition that the story would have to feature the hair oil and promote it. (For details about the competition, see: Bhattacharya, Arupratan. *Bangalir Bigyanbhabana o Sadhana*. Kolkata, Dey's Publishing, 2006.)

While the oil itself was symbolic of the industry of its creator, who was also active in the Swadeshi movement, it was Bose who turns this potentially nationalist symbol to an active cultural symbol that could combine scientific endeavour with nationalist concerns. Bose was the first winner of the competition that would later include some of the best names of the period such as Jagadananda Ray, who wrote what is arguably the first science-fiction story in Bangla (although published much later). Bose later reworked the story for his collection *Abyakto* (1921) with the alternate title 'Palatak Toofan' ('Runaway Cyclone').

The later version has been used for this translation and significant changes have been indicated in the footnotes. Moreover, while the 1896 version uses both English and Bangla, with English for scientific explanation (mostly) and Bangla for the narrative, the 1921 version uses only the latter language. The 1921 version also excludes a long explanatory passage from a scientific journal at the end of the story, as well as a reference to the Empire (both in English).

The source texts for translation of both the 1896 and 1921 versions of the story were taken from *Sera Kalpabigyan* (Best Science Fiction), ed. Anish Deb (Kolkata: Ananda Publishers Limited, 2007). The 1921 version has been cross-checked against the reprinted *Abyakto: A Collection of Popular Science of Jagadish Chandra Bose articles and other essays* by Jagadish Chandra Bose (Kolkata: Dey's Publishing, 2009 [1921]).

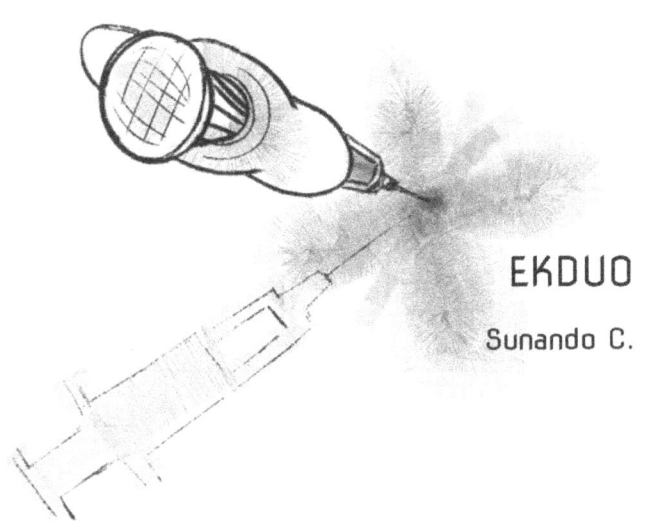

EKDUO

Sunando C.

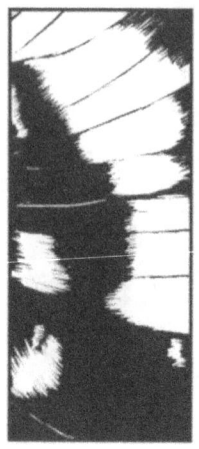 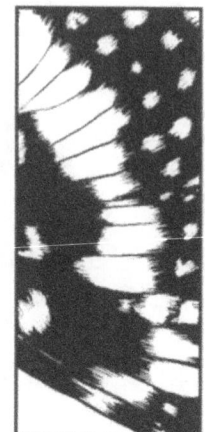 

ekduo

DEPARTMENT OF BIOTECHNOLOGY
(DBT) MINISTRY OF SCIENCE
AND TECHNOLOGY
AWARD FOR EXCELLENCE - 1987

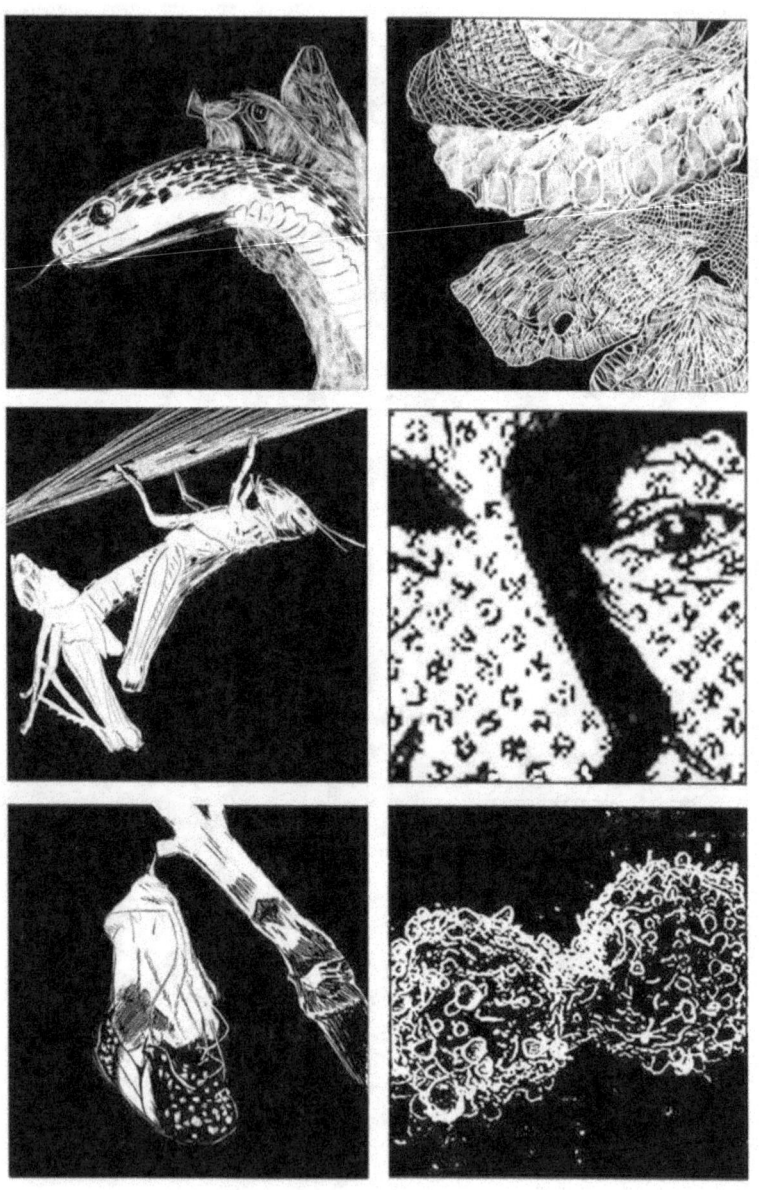

It is with our ... regret that we ... ... untreatable. In ... opi...

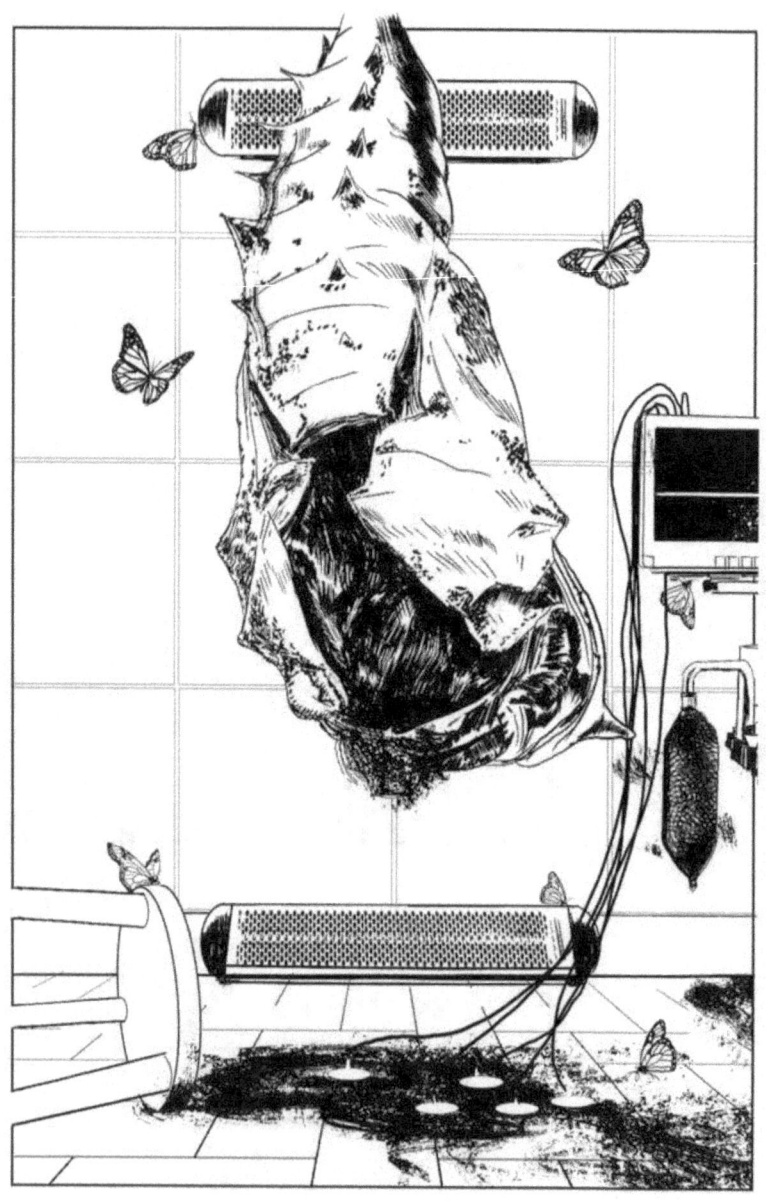

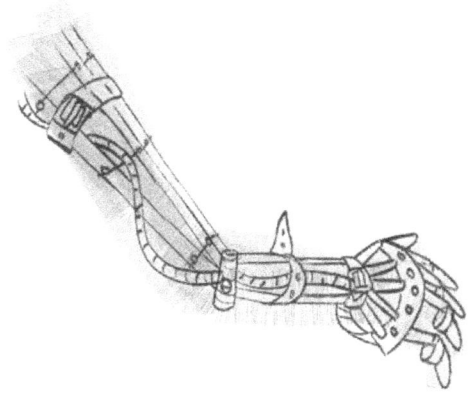

THE LITTLE BEGUM

Indrapramit Das

B ina looked at the metal bones covering her worn and stunted limbs, cold against her legs and feet, lovingly layering the scars of her disease. These new hands and feet were heavy, lead and steel woven with leather straps onto the outside of her body. She had watched her sister Rani make them with fire and scrap, bending the pieces with hammer and heat, her second-hand British goggles flickering with the light of the workshop's tiny forge, sparks flying off her skin as if she were invincible. Bina did not feel invincible wearing them—these skeletal gloves and boots. They trapped her already strength-less arms

'The Little Begum' first appeared in *Steampunk World*, an anthology edited by Sarah Hans and published by Alliteration Ink.

and legs, weighed them down till she felt more helpless that she'd ever been, especially with Rani standing over her, ten years older, so much life in her limbs.

~

'When the Mughal Emperor Shah Jahan's dearest wife Mumtaz died giving birth to their fourteenth child, his grief was so all-consuming he could barely think, let alone rule an empire. So he decided he would build a monument to his grief, to honour the woman who had been so important to him.'

'The Taj Mahal!' said Bina. She knew some history from her time in the boarding houses, and the stories Rani told her. She let Rani go on.

'That's right. Shah Jahan gathered the best craftsmen, the best metal-workers.'

'Like you!' said Bina. Rani smiled and nodded.

'...and the best engineers in his realm, and they built a monument, a metal being to house and guard his wife's body. The Taj Mahal was the greatest automaton ever built: over 300 feet tall, plated in ivory, its massive limbs inlaid with lapis lazuli and onyx and other precious stones, its contours cleverly crafted to look like a palatial tomb when it crouched at rest like a man folded on his knees with his head to Mecca, the spiked tanks on its back raised to the sky like graceful white minarets. To look upon the Taj Mahal walking along the banks of the Yamuna and across the water lapping its metal ankles as if the broad river were a little stream was to see the impossible.

And that's because it was impossible. That metal-and-ivory giant couldn't walk, not even with the most powerful and intricate steam engines and hydraulics built by the empire's best engineers. It would topple and crash before taking a single step. No, it needed a pilot gifted with telekinetic thought to lift its every component, to give it a human soul to go along with the machinery.'

Like me. Bina didn't say, but she realized why her sister was telling her this story.

'Shah Jahan tried piloting it himself. He failed. Very few, after all, are born with the talent of telekinesis, a truth the Emperor did not learn easily. But he did learn it eventually. After scouring the Empire with recruiters, he found, perhaps aptly, that Gauharara Begum, the final daughter Mumtaz had left him with, was the one he was looking for, when one day she lifted an elephant into the air and gently put it down just by looking at it. She was eight at the time, like you. So, with teary eyes, Shah Jahan asked his little daughter Gauharara if she would pilot the walking palace that guarded her mother's remains within its chest. Gauharara said that she would be honoured.'

'And so she did. She was carried by the Emperor's

guards through the winding tunnels of the vast being, past its engines and gears and pipes, past the chamber in its heart that held Gauharara's mother, past its tanks, and she was placed in its head, in a soft cavern of quilted walls. The little Begum made the Taj Mahal walk, looking out of its filigreed eyes to the empire her father ruled, once with the help of her mother. Gauharara Begum took the huge metal-and-ivory beast across the land, with the aid of a faithful crew that ran its engines. The Empire celebrated this wonder amongst them, striding in the distance, with colourful pennants lashing behind it like hair, breathing steam.

But before long, Shah Jahan's third son, Aurangzeb, ordered that the giant never be piloted again, because it was blasphemous to create such automatons, that this lifeless walking idol was a mockery of Allah. Aurangzeb had his father and his beloved Gauharara put under house arrest at the Red Fort in Agra, and after a war of succession with his brothers, became the next Mughal Emperor in a sweeping victory. Shah Jahan died imprisoned, and Gauharara died many years later of old age. Aurangzeb was a devout, efficient Emperor, and oversaw the last years of the Mughal Empire that was. The Emperors who followed led it to its decline, and eventually, they were easily defeated by the British Empire with their airships and tanks. Perhaps if the Mughals had made more automatons to rid the Taj of its solitude, and kept them walking, they'd have kept this land too. They could have thrown airships from the sky, and crushed tanks under their feet. The Taj Mahal never walked again, folding into its rest by the banks of the Yamuna, where to this day its empty tanks gleam like minarets on the horizon, its scalp and shoulders shorn of pennants.'

Bina nodded, looking straight at her sister's grease- and oil-covered face glimmering in the candlelight, at her coarse tattooed hands between her knees. She smiled. Somewhere in the slum, a stray dog barked.

'I know why you told me that story,' Bina said. She wondered if their mother or their father had taught Rani to tell that story. Or both.

'Of course you do. You're a clever girl,' Rani said.

'You told it really well. But it's just really sad,' Bina murmured.

'One day,' her sister said, putting her warm palm on Bina's cheek, 'you're going to see the Taj Mahal at rest by the banks of the Yamuna. You're going to walk, walk with me, and we'll get out of here and go north to see it. Understand?'

Bina shook her head. As if to check, she tried moving her stick-like legs. They barely complied; distant, far-off limbs attached to her body through some unfathomable fog that cut off her brain from their worn-out nerves.

'We're in a slum. We can't get good doctors like the babus and the sahibs. I'm not going to walk. You should stop saying that I will.'

Rani knew not to insist any further. She looked ashamed, which hurt Bina. But she was angry, and didn't say anything. Rani blew out the candle next to the mat and pulled the blanket over Bina, kissing her on the forehead.

~

'Do you remember, Bina, years ago, the first time I told you the story of the Taj Mahal? What I said to you?' Rani asked.

Bina's eyes welled up before she could stop herself. Her legs, weak and immobile and worn away to skin and bones by her sickness, remained that way under the exoskeletal harness her sister had spent hours and days making. All those days, and Bina had thought it was just another project repairing parts for the British and the babus with their various steam-powered machines.

'Am I going to hop in the Taj Mahal and make it walk again? Is that what you want me to do?' Even as Bina asked these questions, she felt her voice rising. She was horrified that she was shouting at her sister after everything she had done for her, but she was.

She couldn't see her sister's reaction through the tears.

'No, Bina,' she laughed, obviously letting her little sister cry without drawing attention to it. 'No. But there's a reason we're all here in this slum, a reason that the British laws don't allow telekinesis for people like us, for everyone who isn't white. There's a reason Aurangzeb, ambitious, devout Aurangzeb, was terrified by his father's creation, and his sister's power. There was a time a little girl made a giant walk. Even if that's not true, even if it was a whole army of telekinetics who made the Taj Mahal walk, that's an impossible feat. It's a miracle. Now I've seen you lift pots and pans with your telekinesis, Bina. I've seen you lift the scrap in my workshop. If you can lift those, you can lift these. They're the same. You're good at it. I know it. You're getting big. You know, you know this. I hate to say this. I can't carry you forever. I wish I could, but I can't.'

'Even if I could move this. If I ever went out, the British would see this skeleton, and they'd kill us probably.'

'I'll cover your hands and feet with cloth, we'll say your limbs are scarred if anyone ever asks. We'll figure it out.'

'I…'

'No,' Rani's voice was suddenly hard. 'No more excuses. I've seen you pick up things with your mind. This harness is a thing. Your arms and legs are in it. You're going to pick them up, and pick up your arms and legs.'

Rani held out her hands. 'Take my hands,' she said. And almost without thinking, Bina did, her exoskeletal fingers grasping at Rani's flesh. Rani held her hands, winced, and pulled her up.

Bina heard the metal joints around her thin legs creak, the straps tighten with new movement like unused muscles, and she felt the pieces of metal in the harness around her float like dust in sunlight, drifting as her mind vanished into a profound numbness, dominated only by the image of a child in a padded chamber, sitting calmly in the centre of her skull. She felt the pieces of metal float and lift her thin legs and arms, which filled with the sparkling tingle of blood moving fresh through their weakened vessels.

She was standing. By herself. Held up by metal, metal held adrift by a little child in her head. The leather soles under her exoskeletal feet squeaked as she nearly fell down in shock, but corrected herself.

Rani watched, her mouth open, arms held out to grab her sister if she fell.

Bina was shivering violently.

'My little Begum,' Bina said softly, her voice trembling ever so slightly. 'Come forward.'

'I can't move,' Bina said, voice thick.

'Why?'

'I...I'm scared,' she said.

'My Begum. I know. I know. But I'm here. I won't let

you fall. Just look, look at your hands. Look what they're doing.'

Bina looked at her hands, at the metal fingers flexing and unflexing by her side, their parts moving and clicking, joints bending, blessing her deformed fingers with intricate movement. 'Oh, god,' Bina said. The metal fingers seized, stopped their clicking.

'Don't,' Rani said. 'You're thinking too much. You were moving them without even thinking of it.'

'Okay,' Bina whispered.

'Bina. You're standing. You haven't done that in years. Don't be afraid.' Bina thought of the years and years of being curled in her sister's powerful arms, letting the sun warm her face on their morning walks by the river.

'I'll fall if I move,' Bina said.

'I'm here if you do.'

Rani took off her necklace and held it out. 'Use your fingers. Take it.'

Her hand shook as she raised it. She watched the little gears spin in the joints, the fingers bending to grasp the necklace. She held it in between her metal fingers. 'Wear it,' Rani said. Her arms floated up, her hands passing her head, and she felt the necklace around her neck. It was a string tied to a featureless coin their father had hammered, to practice telekinesis with their mother, passing it between their hands through the air. Bina didn't remember this herself. The coin hung against her chest.

'That's it. You're doing better than I could have ever hoped.'

Bina nodded. She closed her eyes, and pennants unfurled from her scalp in the sunlight flashing off her great ivory-plated shoulders. She breathed in deep, felt the giant bellows in her, the furnaces in her torso flare with life. Felt the entire engine of her machinery close around the twin tombs deep inside her, protecting them. She breathed out, steam rushing from the ports on her head and back, gushing ribbons of cloud into the pale sky. Her hands were huge, big enough to pick up cattle, elephants. Underneath her was their entire slum, sprawled across the banks of the Hooghly, in the distance the white palatial city of the British, of Calcutta, airships hovering like balloons above it, tethered to the land with strings she could snap with her fingers. An army of British soldiers couldn't stop her. They'd flee, or be crushed, their bullets glancing harmlessly off her towering body.

'We'll travel?' Bina asked, her voice breaking.

'We will. We'll go to Delhi. We'll find a way to get you new medicine. We'll see the Taj Mahal. I promise.'

Bina felt dizzy, her own height strange to her. She heard her metal fingers clicking again, moving again. Flexing. Unflexing. She thought of the little Begum pilot in the padded chamber in her skull, her resolve, looking out at the world through the windows of a giant's eyes. This little Begum didn't have an Emperor for a father, and a dead Empress for a mother. In fact, she was no Begum, just a girl. This little girl had a father and mother who were metal-workers, who were shot by the British when it was discovered they were both telekinetic. This little girl had a sister with whom she was sent to be 'civilized' in an imperial boarding house. This little girl had a sister who had kept them both alive over years on the streets, had found them refuge working metal like their parents had in a slum where people went to die because it was cheap; a sister who kept her alive when she fell sick, and stayed sick.

Bina felt a fire in those bellows in her chest, burning, licking at the massive grinding gears. She closed her metal hands into fists. She thought of the little girl in her skull, and this time there was an older girl beside her—her sister, safe inside the padded chamber, looking out across the empire through those huge windowed eyes, that empire once Mughal, now British, perhaps one day something else entirely. They looked out together, to the snap and flutter of pennants catching the wind outside. The little girl would keep her sister safe in that chamber.

'Walk, Bina,' said her sister. So she did.

THE MONSTER AT THE END
OF PHYSICS

Shalini Srinivasan

When Dasappa told people the story of the night the smallest of the seven dolmens turned black, he liked to make it clear it was Physics: 'Don't think it was some ghost and all,' he would say. 'It was proper science. A giant magnet built to attract the stars. And it did. You should've seen how many stars fell from the sky that night! Like god was setting off fireworks! They were even in the newspaper the next day.'

Meena never talked about that night. The closest she came was in her refusal to drive motor vehicles, and her lifelong hatred for study holidays.

~

The first time Meena heard her own voice echo through the hole at the back of the smallest dolmen, she was lying on the hill. Light fuzzed around the pale hair on the stalks of a wild balsam near her face and made everything feel vague and dreamlike. She didn't realize it was her own voice until some weeks later, but she did recognize it as familiar, and her hair stood up on her arms. Meena closed her eyes. The sun was orange and red inside her eyelids, and she wondered if maybe her father was right and what she needed was therapy, some kind of violent sport, and a good, tough study schedule to keep her body tired and her imagination in check.

The second time Meena heard the voice, she had been on a studying streak. Though she lay on the dolmen, her mind was reciting integration formulae, so she knew it was too full to be whimsical. Yet there was the voice, mumbling something about penguins. That was when a familiar resentment inched its way across her face. She decided her father was wrong and that her imagination was quite enough in check. Her studying mood crumbled and blew away. Meena wondered, over the next couple of days, if maybe she'd prefer it if her father were right. At least he had a plan for life, even if it was a rubbish one.

The third time, the voice was barely there, a hint of breeze through the hole. It sounded a lot like her mother, which was unfair. Two parents in a day was too many.

Meena had just got a letter from her father that morning, hoping she had finished at least two rounds of syllabus revisions, and trusting that she was going to be responsible and adult and—her least favourite word—*reasonable.* Not surprisingly, she was feeling unstable and dangerous as she climbed up to the dolmens. When the voice came through the smallest dolmen, faint, vague, present only in the rise and fall of its sentences, she imagined a fuse being lit at one end of her nose. That was the time she decided to maybe blow everything up.

~

Twelfth standard had not been kind to Meena, and Meena had been unkind right back to it. Her Physics teacher had burst into tears twice after the last exam: once when giving Meena back her answer paper, and once when handing it to her father and reminiscing about back when Meena hadn't yet declared war on her life. Meena had stayed stony on both occasions and took her punishment with a shrug.

Being banished to Vijaya Aunty's farmhouse was not Meena's idea of a punishment—despite the general feeling among bus conductors and co-passengers that anyone who could live in Cantonment and instead travelled into the countryside to live among the accumulated debris of 2,000-plus years of skirmishing deserved to be killed by a yakshi wearing their face. Meena hadn't been very upset to get away from home, but she cheered right up at mention of the yakshi. The bus deposited her at the feet of a dusty neem tree, and there was Vijaya Aunty: sari pleats haphazard, left chappal fraying, and voice very kind. They trudged down a dust path, taking turns to drag Meena's suitcase. Meena searched Vijaya Aunty's face closely for signs of supernatural evil. Instead, Vijaya Aunty was all too human: vague, preoccupied, and amazingly uninterested in what Meena did with her studying time.

Meena's mother had always gone on about the wonderful vegetables Vijaya Aunty grew. Recent events suggested that Meena's mother was not entirely to be trusted. As far as Meena could tell, Vijaya Aunty mostly farmed rocks: lumps of granite and gneiss in a variety of sizes and shapes stuck out of the hillside around the farmhouse, making for excellent climbing and napping and hiding. Bits of forts and walls and pillars stuck out here and there; lapwings nested in the occasional curve of some decayed mandapam. The vegetable fields were flat little emerald-and-garnet patches tucked away between the rocks. According to Dasappa, they were lush and fertile with the blood of a thousand battles—and ploughing season yielded a bounty of spear-heads and bones and bits of armour, even sophisticated bullets from the recent caste wars. Meena's favourite things were the dolmens, a set of seven that some long-dead people had built on top of the hill. The architecture was simple: three slabs set in a U for the walls, one large slab over them like a roof. Smaller stones bolstered up the dolmens, and plugged in the gaps, leaving a peephole at the back. Though the dry season had started, water seeped through them off and on, leaving dark mossy trails across the rock. The top of the hill was only a couple of hundred feet above Vijaya Aunty's house, but every now and then a wild wind swept errant crows screaming across it, making it feel like another world. Meena had begun to wonder if the dolmens were in fact somehow haunted; they appeared to be, at the very least, in a different climate zone from the rest of the village. And they smelt wrong.

She asked Dasappa about it. Dasappa was the local wise man. He had survived elephants stomping his crops, king cobras adopting his bathrooms, and leopards stalking his sheep; he knew a vast amount of gossip about what plant could cure what ailment, and the scandalous doing of an enormous number of personages dead, alive, and mythical. If you asked Dasappa, he could locate every word of every Jataka and the Mahabharata in and around the village. For instance, he told Meena that the Pandavas hadn't *really* gone off to heaven via the Himalayas, as befitted good local boys. They had climbed to the top of their very own hill, the dolmens marking where each fell.

Dasappa knew every inch of the landscape, and he talked about it as if it were a person—the bolthole where the last rat of the 1534 plague had sheltered; the rocks under which Tipu Sultan had hidden a vast treasure and a cannon that could shoot across the ocean and destroy London; the wall Rajamma built to keep an amorous chieftain away from her herb garden and her virtue; the dent made by a chatty turtle falling from a great height; the cave in which Rani Chennamma had once stayed the night on a campaign—which was on other days the cave in which immortal Jambavan still lived; the banyan tree that was part of a vast complex that once extended from the Kaveri to the Tungabhadra; the small dolmen where Chandru's double had once appeared and beat him up before turning toothpastey and squeezing back in through the peephole at the back.

Meena wondered if she would figure in Dasappa's stories.

~

It was Chandru who was on Meena's mind that morning, a few weeks into her study holidays. *First foray,* she told herself as she climbed over broken wall bits and around some ancient quarry. She walked past the pale pink balsams that were 50 per cent of the population of the dolmen hill and crawled into the smallest of the seven dolmens. It had a small porthole on one end, and its lichens were a hideous and marvellous orange-and-grey-and-green, set in overlapping circles that made Meena vaguely uneasy if she stared at them too long.

And then Meena did something truly stupid. She set up a lightning rod, hoping to catch bubbles of other universes, other Meenas. She suspected that the dolmens attracted them.

There was no lightning that day, so Meena had to re-plan.

The truth was that Meena wasn't failing 12th-standard Physics because she didn't understand it; Meena was failing 12th-standard Physics because she didn't want to pass it. She believed that in a next-door universe, somewhere, a Meena was passing Physics fine. Kidnapping this parallel-universe version of herself to pass an exam she had no interest in was the kind of physics Meena was willing to work at.

One week later, it turned out that it was the kind of physics Meena was excellent at.

~

Meena's plans came together mostly unconsciously. She asked lot of questions, circling always around the dolmens.

She asked about the people who saw their own faces, she asked about Chandru's double, she asked about the whens and the hows and the what-were-they-wearings. Meena soon came to the conclusion that night-time was best, and that some kind of unavoidable astronomical event would be useful. She read about fungal networks in the forest, and began to suspect that the mosses in the dolmens stretched into other worlds. She 'borrowed' several iron diggers, she asked everyone she met about doubles. She spent a lot of time among the dolmens, and she began to think she could hear faint echoes.

~

One week later, Meena was on foray number two and the story of Chandru still lingered in her head. This time, she had made a lot of preparations, and discarded most of them. She told Vijaya Aunty she was borrowing her tractor to drive up and watch the meteor shower that was due that night.

'Physics,' she added. This was both true and some world-class   lying-by-omission-of-the-rest-of-the-sentence. The Yudhishtira dolmen would have been proud of her, Meena thought. By then Meena was half-wishing Vijaya Aunty would ask her some questions, maybe ground her a little.

'Ah,' said Vijaya Aunty. 'Yes, yes.' She went back to her ledger: clearly the economics of farming rocks and ruins and nine varieties of endangered brinjal was more interesting than the ramifications of underage driving. Meena was unsurprised.

Meena drove the tractor up the hill, and to the dolmens, and began her preparations.

By the time night fell, the smallest dolmen (either Sahadeva or Yama-as-Yudhishtira's dog, depending on who you asked) looked like a porcupine: crouched darkly on the hillside, and bristling with iron rods. Meena had stuck a variety of iron things into it—diggers, spade-handles, the large-toothed plough. Then she hooked the tractor engine to an alternator. Meena sat at its entrance, half in, half out, one leg stretching into the sand inside and one dangling out. If she turned left, she could see the sky through the peephole at the back of the dolmen; if she turned right, the hill sloped down to the farmhouse. It seemed somehow significant.

The meteor shower started slowly, a tiny suggestion of a line across the sky. Then it sped up, brightened. More streaks appeared, gold and white and dust. A large pinkish streak made its slow sure way across the sky. Meena jumped up and ran to the tractor and turned on the engine. Then she ran back to her post and flung herself down, half expecting the power to fry her.

It didn't. Meena leaned back and looked for the pink meteor. Through the hole in the dolmen, the sky was subtly different, the air a little thicker, a little more orange than she was used to. The long meteor streak had tilted right and down and was touching the horizon, two shorter ones just above it.

'You!' said a voice, and it sounded so like her mother that Meena found herself up, running and then sinking when her knees gave up, everything trembling with adrenaline and horror, muttering over and over, *I fucking hate study holidays.*

Some distant part of her was aware that she was being unfair, and that her current status (Mortal peril. Possibly.) was entirely her own fault. But she blamed the plan on the jittery-yet-expansive mood her study holidays gave her, expectation, nerves and possibility strung together and twanged loose and tight by her sudden freedom from home and the hated school schedule, and by the glorious expanse of wilderness that stretched around her.

As Meena clutched her knees, trembling and swearing at study holidays, she began to imagine what it was she had done. Had she made an electro-magnet? A radio transmitter? Or a lightning rod? What kind of thing had she attracted?

The air was rank with burning things. Meena's hair had melted off. She concentrated on the soft slow steps coming toward her, unable now to do anything except wait for it.

'Are you...?' the voice asked, so much like someone she knew.

'Amma?' Meena asked, closing her eyes. She didn't think she could bear it.

The footsteps stopped. Then nothing moved for a while. Meena opened her eyes and watched the large pinkish meteor trail began to fade. Her legs stopped trembling. Finally, Meena turned and met the translucent peeled-grape eyes that belonged to the voice so like her mother's. Her own.

'Why did *you* call me here?' Other Meena asked. She still sounded like Amma had, but Meena now noticed differences: she was looser, more mumbly. Was this what her own voice was like outside her head? Other Meena lifted an eyebrow. It was normal too. Apparently only her eyes had evolved from snot. Veiny, palely bloody snot. Meena felt sick. She settled for rubbing violently at her own eyes, now throbbing in sympathy.

'Why?' Other Meena repeated.

Meena said lightly, 'I wanted you to write my Physics exam.'

Other Meena replied, quick as a cat. 'If you write my Chem.'

They nodded. It seemed fair.

The tractor engine roared on, and the air smelt sharp and salty, and slightly sick with petrol. Other Meena's face was drawn in thin jagged lines, and her mouth allowed for no pity. There was nowhere to hide.

'How is Amma?' Meena asked. A question to cross universes for.

The other Meena's face crumbled in, and the horrible revolting truth, the reason why Other Meena had been waiting at the dolmen became suddenly obvious.

'I don't want to go home,' they both said.

'I thought I'd come to yours instead,' Meena said. 'Just…see her while you did my exam.'

Other Meena nodded, 'So did I.'

'I guess she's the same, then,' Meena said, more comment than question.

Other Meera shrugged, a twitch of one shoulder that made her look very old. She climbed to the top of the dolmen and sat down to watch the meteors. Meena joined her, stone cold even through her jeans. She thought it was the least possible price to pay for universe-level meddling. Other Meena watched her for two or three long minutes, and then turned away. Meenas didn't like to talk, and just then they were glad for the company. They sat there for a long time, completely silent.

~

In the years after, Dasappa always told the story of how he found Meena asleep, maybe knocked-out, on top of the dolmen the next morning. She and the dolmen were oily-black with soot. Meena's hair was frizzed to the roots. The moss and lichens were charred. The various iron implements rusted as if they had lived a thousand years in that one night. Only Meena's eyes were pale and see-through, some kind of reverse charring, and she squinted unfamiliarly at Dasappa as if unable to recognize him in the haze. Or maybe the sight was burnt out of them by all th.e stars.

The tractor battery was terribly dead, and its engine burnt hollow, never to recover. The air, he would tell everyone, stank of scorched hair and petrol, and salt and sulphur, as if someone had set off a small bomb on their own head. It was so dreadful even the wind couldn't seem to dissipate it.

Dasappa always ended the story by waving his hand out into the universe in a generous and expansive gesture. 'That was the night the stars fell,' he said. 'The poor child! Her mother had just gone off to see the stars for the next forty years, you know—Vijaya's sister, she was. Exploring Space, it seems! So that child, she built a giant machine to pull the stars to Earth. Paapa, she thought her mother would follow them and come back. I'll never forget her eyes after, peeled and bleached. And for what? Her mother never did return.'

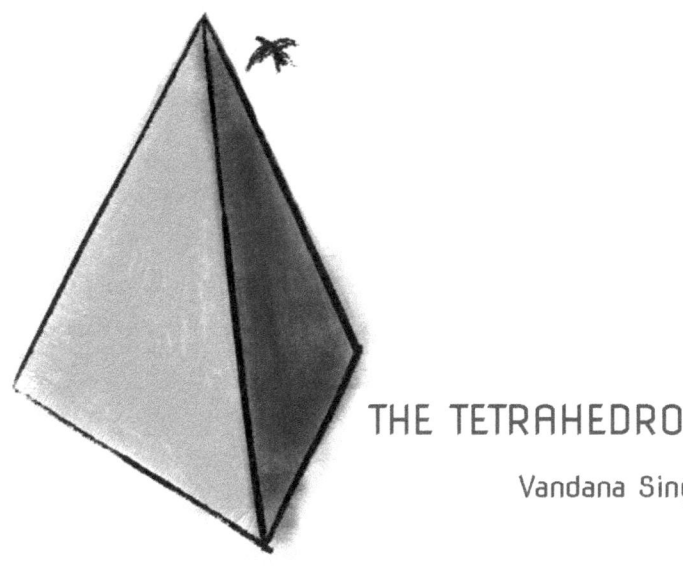

THE TETRAHEDRON

Vandana Singh

The story of the Tetrahedron—its mysterious appearance in the middle of a busy street in New Delhi, India—is known in the remotest corners of the globe. There are pictures of it everywhere, towering over the trees and buildings while an anonymous crowd stands outside the fenced area, staring up at it in awe. But few know the story of one of the witnesses of this extraordinary event—an apparently ordinary young woman by the name of Maya, who stood waiting at a bus-stop near the intersection known as Patel Chowk on the fateful morning when the Tetrahedron first appeared. To understand her story we

---

'The Tetrahedron' was previously published in *The Woman Who Thought She Was a Planet and Other Stories* (Zubaan/Penguin India; 2009).

must look upon her with the gaze of someone who cares, so she becomes more than a face in the crowd. The way her brother Manoj considers her, perhaps, when he imagines her standing at the bus-stop at the start of it all—the thin, heart-shaped face, the wistful curiosity in her brown eyes, like a child in a china shop who has been told not to touch things...

She was dressed in a somewhat gaudy red patchwork tunic over narrow black trousers; a cloth bag hung over her shoulder, declaring her unequivocally a student of Delhi University. She was late for Accounting class, had long since given up hope of arriving in time, and was therefore letting buses bound for the University pass her by. It was this philosophical resignation, and her preoccupation with her thoughts, cantered at that moment on her fiancé, Mr Perfect Kartik, that resulted in her witnessing the manifestation (for lack of a better word) of the Tetrahedron.

She stood a little apart from the crowds at the bus-stop: young, sleek-headed men with cell-phones, steely-eyed women in saris carrying brief-cases, students in a colourful knot discussing politics. It was a cool morning in February and the crows were hunched on the neem trees over her head, watching the peanut-seller with beady eyes. The air smelled of traffic fumes and roasting peanuts, and somebody's flowery perfume.

What she was thinking about at this moment was how Kartik was beginning to irritate her. Maya's engagement to Kartik represented her final surrender to the demands of respectability. Every foray she had made into the out-of-the-ordinary—playing cricket with the boys, climbing trees, buying an entire tray of bangles from a beggar girl in the market, making friends with the girl in the next apartment block who rode a motorbike and was reputed to be 'wild'—had been met with parental consternation, lectures on family honour and marital prospects, and had left her with busloads of guilt. So she felt like a traitor even thinking about how Kartik was starting to annoy her...

Lately, whenever she met Kartik (under the watchful eyes of some elderly relative or other) he would lecture her on her failings. The halwa she had made for tea was a little too sweet, that sari was a little flashy—and by the way, could she bring him the newspaper? But the worst was the way her mother and father acted around Kartik, as though he were some minor deity that must be kept in a constant state of appeasement. If only her brother Manoj, two years her senior, had been there—he would understand, but he had escaped many years ago. He was in the Merchant Navy, stationed now in Vishakhapatnam. Her three elder married sisters were harried mothers and quite useless. As for her friends in college, Maya no longer found their obsession with the latest fashions, jewellery and eligible young men diverting. These days she had been feeling very much alone.

At precisely 10:23 a.m. IST, her musings were interrupted by the appearance of an enormous Tetrahedron in the middle of the street before her. It came suddenly and incongruously into existence—a monstrous black thing, about two stories high, broad enough on its triangular base to span all four lanes of the road. There was a chorus of screeches as cars and scooters and motor-rickshaws braked in desperation, and then a series of prolonged metallic crashes as vehicles behind them made contact. A woman near Maya dropped her bag and began screaming.

Curses, exclamations, invocations to various gods, the sounds of running feet as a stampede began—then a fearful, wondering silence fell upon the crowds that remained on the sidewalk and the people emerging slowly from the vehicles. Even those who had started to run slowed down and turned back to stare. Faces peered out of windows in the building on both sides of the street. The crows themselves stood silent on the branches of the old trees.

Astonishingly, nothing had crashed into the Tetrahedron itself, which stood quietly in the street. To Maya's amazement it seemed as though the two buses, the cars and bicycles that had been in the place now occupied by the Tetrahedron had simply ceased to be.

Moments later Maya found herself walking towards the Tetrahedron with a straggle of other bold onlookers. They stood gazing at its opaque sleekness, its geometrical perfection, wondering, but too afraid to touch. Until a small street urchin held out a dirty hand and touched the thing; then everyone followed suit, patting and feeling the smooth, unyielding surface. Behind them the crowd grew as people emerged from cars and buses to gaze open-mouthed at this unexpected sight and proffer theories. Depending on which religion the theorist professed, it was a signal from the gods that the end of the era of kalyug was here, and destruction was imminent, or that the one true God was about to emerge and pass judgement on the sinners... It was a government ploy (from a disgruntled clerk who refused to speculate as to how or why). It was a bomb from a neighbouring country that would explode any minute now and why were they standing there anyway. It was a new secret weapon the government had developed. It was an invasion by Martians (from a boy in school uniform) or by Egyptians (from his friend, who was contradicted by another schoolboy: 'It's a tetrahedron, not a pyramid, stupid!'). Arguments broke out regarding the possible validity of each theory. Some bemoaned the fate of the people who had been in the space occupied by the Tetrahedron. They must lie crushed flat under this monstrous thing, they said, shaking their heads ghoulishly.

Well, well, who knew where you'd end up when you left your doorstep of a morning?

Then the press came, eager-eyed TV cameramen, the All India Radio people, and, following at their heels, the police. The latter were rather at a loss—there was nothing in the Indian Penal Code about this. The police officer fell back on old ground and began waving his baton at the crowd, 'Move on, you're obstructing traffic!' while some responded, 'What about that thing, it's obstructing traffic, are you going to arrest it?' But finally, in the anarchistic, reluctant way of a large beast, the crowd was pushed back and railings set up around the Tetrahedron. Sirens wailed discordantly while stalled traffic was diverted, and finally army trucks rolled in. Soldiers leaped out and took their places with clockwork precision, rifles agleam, but the Tetrahedron answered no questions or challenges. On the sidewalks a large crowd still stood and stared, and pickpockets and vendors of spicy and sticky concoctions did a roaring trade. Maya was interviewed by a reporter from *The Statesman* ('Did you really touch it? What do you think it might be?').

When she went home (who could sit in a class after this?) her parents were watching the whole thing on TV. The TV was blaring because her mother had the sewing machine going, trying to finish an order from the tailoring shop where she worked. The youngest of her married older sisters, who was here for a visit, was cooking something in the tiny kitchen of the flat, while her firstborn, little Chanchal, babbled in her grandfather's lap. Maya's parents were horrified when she told them she had been there and had touched the thing, but when she mentioned that *The Statesman* had actually interviewed her, their horror knew no bounds. What would Kartik say?

Fortunately Kartik did not subscribe to *The Statesman*. When he came for tea on the following weekend, he talked at length about the Tetrahedron, unaware that Maya had actually been there when it appeared. Kartik's theory was that it was a Pakistani secret weapon. Gratified by the attention of his hosts (his future father-in-law had nodded several times) he grew expansive, dandled little Chanchal on his knee (ignoring her outraged cries) and gave Maya a significant look. Maya, lost in thoughts of her own, stared blankly back at him, although her sister gave her a dig in the ribs and blushed and simpered. Maya had cause to be distracted.

The day after the Appearance, she had gone back to the Tetrahedron as though pulled by an invisible string. There were officious looking policemen guarding it from the public and a small army contingent occupying an entire block. Within the cordon, a group of people had been busy with instruments, in the important, oblivious manner of scientists. Among them she recognized Samir, a Ph.D. student of Astrophysics, who sometimes used the same University bus as Maya. He had once been introduced to her by an acquaintance on the bus, and she remembered his intense, intelligent gaze sweeping over her then with no more than a polite interest.

She had gone over to the cordon and called impulsively out to him, to his considerable surprise—but he was just finished and it had been only natural to go to the University together and to talk about the whole thing at the tea-shack. Nursing her tea in the chipped glass, Maya had told Samir about her witnessing of the Tetrahedron's arrival. 'It didn't arrive,' she'd said, 'I didn't see it come down from the sky, or through the trees. One moment it wasn't there, and the next moment it was.' Samir had listened with great interest.

Now, as she poured Kartik more tea (the best Darjeeling her parents could buy), she thought about the past two days of drinking strong, cheap masala chai with Samir on the old wooden benches in front of the tea-shack. She imagined her parents' shock and horror. What would Kartik say to that?

Samir had told her that the night before the arrival of the Tetrahedron there had been an unusual event—a series of radio pulses from the vicinity of an ordinary yellow star that was not known for such activity. He hypothesized that the Tetrahedron was an alien device, travelling at near-light-speed through space via some unknown mechanism. He was disarmingly frank about his bias towards an astronomical origin for the Tetrahedron—he was a student of Astrophysics after all—but next to the Pakistani-American secret-weapon theory, the astronomical one was the most popular. The people whose relatives had been in the buses and cars that had disappeared were demanding a complete investigation of every possibility. Foreign scientists had flocked to Delhi in droves, as had New Age groupies, end-of-the-world cults, members of the international press and ordinary gawking tourists. The President of the United States had been restrained with difficulty from declaring war on India for possessing secret weapons of mass destruction, and had only been placated with promises of a substantial American presence among the investigators. Other suspicious governments from the West had also sent their representatives. Suddenly New Delhi had become one of the most popular travel destinations in the world. Maya and Samir had laughed over newspaper headlines—the government was building more hotels! The Western press was floundering, unused as they were to reporting anything but disasters and political unrest from the third world! A tabloid reported that India had been chosen for a special reason by a wise alien race, and would shortly receive a message of epic importance concerning the next elections!

But what Maya relived most often in her mind was the feeling when she had touched the Tetrahedron—the feeling of how useless and insignificant her life was against the unending mystery of the universe. Now, with Samir talking eloquently about aliens traversing the distances between stars, she had felt it again, the pointlessness of a life lived small. In a few years she would be like her sisters, plump and resigned, children running at her feet while Kartik gazed benignly at her from the sofa over the evening paper. 'Maya, you know that sari does not suit you...' Maya this and Maya that. Could she take a lifetime of it?

Of course, she had only herself to blame, choosing Kartik. Her parents had left the final choice up to her, from an army of eligible bachelors of the appropriate class and caste. Dressed in her best, serving tea to a succession of potential in-laws and their self-conscious offspring, she had been dazzled by Kartik's assurance. Her parents had approved whole-heartedly. Kartik had a good future in a small company that manufactured shoes, and his parents' flat was huge—large enough to accommodate a young, married couple. But now she was no longer sure of her feelings.

She stopped going to class. Every day she went dutifully to the University, where she hung around the tea-shop, waiting for Samir, listening to old film songs that the proprietor, Ramu, insisted on playing loudly on the radio. They drank strong tea in ancient glasses that had seen better days, and speculated about the Tetrahedron. The scientists had found nothing. The object was made out of an unbelievably hard substance that could not be chipped off for testing. X-rays bounced merrily off it. It was much too heavy to be moved (this to the disappointment of an American software billionaire who wanted to transport it to his mansion in the US). Neither controlled explosives nor corrosive chemicals had the slightest effect on it. Digging under it for the remains of the unfortunate bus and car passengers, the authorities found nothing—no bodies, no crushed bones or flesh, no evidence of charred remains, just dirt and the impenetrable substance of the Tetrahedron standing over it. It stood implacable, a question with no answer.

~

When she was not at the tea-shop, Maya began to spend her time gawking at the Tetrahedron with the large crowd that was always there. Like others in the crowd, she felt as though she, too, was waiting for something. The road where the Tetrahedron stood was now blocked to traffic, of course, and its immediate vicinity was patrolled by a now international team of soldiers on permanent alert.

Meanwhile a series of shops had sprung up overnight in the parking lot of an adjacent building. Soft drinks, tea, hot samosas, cameras, film, knick-knacks such as plastic replicas of the Tetrahedron were being sold at exorbitant prices. Foreign languages from all over the world mingled with radio music from the shops and live commentary from TV station crewmen. Rich businessmen rubbed shoulders with hippies and street urchins; Americans and Middle-Easterners, Japanese, Koreans, Kenyans all stood gawking and chattering in little groups. People-watching became Maya's hobby. Her favourite pastime was to eavesdrop on the conversations that sprang up in her vicinity—fragments of arguments, discussions, both academic and untutored—it was a feast for the ears.

'...the heat, the dust... Why here?'

'...the weapons theory has been more or less defused by now, no pun intended...except for the politicians, paranoid as usual...'

'Beats me... Place wasn't even what I expected. No elephants, or dancing girls, or any of that shit.... Got my camcorder along and for what... All that thing does is to sit there while we sweat our butts off.'

'Reason...there's a reason it's special, if you read the paper by MacArthur...'

'...and they don't even eat monkey heads, man, so much for Indiana Jones...bunch of vegetarians...'

'Don't grumble, dear, it was your idea…'

'…what do you expect Hollywood to do, make documentaries…'

'Well, the Johnsons, they went all over this country… couldn't stand their boasting…'

'…the term synchronicity? Meaningful coincidence…'

'…got some shots of the cows on the roads, weird enough for me…'

'…yes, like when you're thinking of a song and the DJ starts playing it—what's that got to do with…'

'…even the fast food joints aren't the same…'

'…only in a place like this, look at the traffic. By Western standards, with conditions like this, most people ought to be dead or dying. What keeps them going, eh? How anything functions here is a small miracle. A modification of the Jungian concept of synchronicity…'

'…did you hear what happened to the Gustafsons? The hotel didn't have any record of their reservations, poor things. They ended up you'll never guess where…'

'…Never in Japan, no. Far more disciplined people. There's something in the air over here, as though the chaos is intrinsic to the place…'

'…in the home of the student they'd hosted ten years ago, back when they were in Tucson…'

'…dimensional anomalies…fellow called Bhaskar, native—I mean Indian mathematician, cosmologist…yes, in the *Times*...no, no, the *London Times*...theorizes that dimensional anomalies must exist in this region, hence the Tetrahedron...'

'...intrinsic anarchy, I like that, no wonder we couldn't hold on to the Empire...'

Maya would listen, fascinated. Sometimes a tourist would come up to her and ask if she'd agree to be photographed in front of the Tetrahedron. She was always discomfited by these requests and would back away with a muttered 'sorry'. Mostly she kept a low profile, watching, listening, sipping a drink or two, letting her thoughts drift, wondering at the silence, the serenity of the Tetrahedron in the midst of all the noise and bustle.

At home, nobody guessed what was going on in Maya's head as she pounded spices in the little kitchen, or hung wet laundry on the nylon clothesline in the balcony. In the evenings, the tiny flat was full of the sound of the sewing machine. Her mother's scissors went snip-snip as iridescent piles of cloth accumulated on the drawing-room floor. She would put some of the bright cloth aside to make a dress for Chanchal or a patchwork salwaar kameez for Maya. Her customers never found out. 'Your mother is a marvel,' her father said one day, when the dress was ready. 'She can add two and two and get five!'

'Dimensional anomalies!' Maya said with a small smile, and went into the kitchen to wash dishes. She gazed moodily out of the window at a view of rooftops and TV antennas, crowded streets, music and conversations blaring from tiers of lit open windows—over all this, in a hazy, dark sky, glimmered a faint star or two. Maya wondered what she was going to do with her life.

Tea with Kartik. Endless teas and breakfasts and dinners with Kartik. When he came the next evening he looked tired and a little vulnerable, and she felt a small pang. But seeing her parents bustling about him, deferring to his every wish, she felt her old irritation arise again. To make matters worse Kartik started talking about the Tetrahedron. This time he was convinced China had something to do with it too. After all, why stop at Pakistan? Maya set the teapot on the table down so loudly that everyone stopped talking and stared at her in amazement.

'What do you know about it?' she snapped at Kartik. Her heart was hammering in her chest. She was conscious for a moment that she was opening a door she would not be able to shut again. But her anger and confusion, held back as long as it had been, surged over what was left of common sense.

'China! Pakistan! Has it occurred to you that nobody— not anybody—can understand what that thing is? None of the foreign scientists, none of ours. Can't you see anything outside your own damned backyard?'

She turned on her heel and went into the kitchen, shaking violently, leaving a dead silence behind her.

Then a clink as her mother set down her cup, and her apologetic voice saying desperately to Kartik, 'Please understand, she is just...you know, sometimes young women...that time of the month...she doesn't mean it...'

And her father now beside her, looking at her in shock and hurt, saying, 'What have you done, child?'

What had she done? Insulted the man who was going to be her husband, damaged the fragile alliance between Kartik's parents and her own, lowered the family honour by behaving like a squabbling fish-wife instead of a girl from a respectable family. She looked at her father's upset face, at his shoulders stooping from disappointment, and burst into tears. She went blindly into the room she shared with her visiting sister and the child. Her sister patted her head.

'Listen, you donkey, that is no way to behave before marriage. You can quarrel all you want afterwards; look at Ashish and me—I shout at him all the time...'

'I don't want to marry Kartik,' she said between sobs. It was a relief to have said it at last. But she could hear her parents in the drawing room, anxiously trying to placate Kartik. She heard his chair scrape on the floor as he rose, heard him say, 'I hope I have not been mistaken in her. If she comes to her senses...'

Then the front door shut.

After that, for some days, she really tried. She hadn't understood before how vulnerable her parents were, how frightened at the thought that their youngest daughter might never get married. Three daughters had slowly depleted them of their meagre savings, and Kartik's family had not even asked for gifts (the euphemism for the illegal dowry). They'd never find anyone like him. So the very next day she went to the phone booth at the corner of her street, called Kartik and apologized rather stiffly. He did not say anything except to tell her that he was going out of town on business for two weeks, and he would think about this when he returned.

Three days of attending classes and bearing with the questions of her friends put her in such a black depression that she returned to Patel Chowk. One day when the square seemed particularly crowded, she fought her way to the edge near the parking area, clutching her soft drink in her hand, to stand beneath the generous shade of an ancient tree. It was then that she noticed a white van marked with the words 'Ravindra Refrigeration Systems' parked near her. It looked familiar—she must have seen it there before without really noticing it. The side door of the van was open and a motley group of people were gathered around it, talking.

They were all so different from each other that it took

her a moment to realize they were a group—three elderly men, two young women who looked Japanese, a lean young man who could have been from the Middle East, and most incongruous of them all, an old lady in a beige salwaar-kameez perched in the open doorway of the van, knitting away. There was something indefinably different about them compared to the rest of the crowd—they seemed relaxed, they hardly glanced at the Tetrahedron, they spoke to each other in low, easy tones.

Maya wondered why she had never really noticed them before. But the Tetrahedron attracted so many kinds of people that perhaps it was no wonder. Now someone with a loudspeaker was shouting; policemen were pushing the crowds aside with batons. Another politician? No, it was a movie star, said a plump woman in a purple sari excitedly to Maya. Look, Malini Mehra herself in a glittering pink sari with a daring backless blouse, at the souvenir booth, waving flirtatiously at the gawking, camera-clicking onlookers. Maya turned away in exasperation. There, behind the trees, was the Tetrahedron, the cause of all the excitement. As she glanced at its pinnacle rising into the sky above the treetops, she thought she saw one of the ubiquitous crows flying directly towards it. What was the bird doing? She squinted up at it but the sun was in her eyes. She thought she saw the bird reach one edge of the Tetrahedron; then it disappeared.

She rubbed her eyes and blinked. The plump woman was still beside her, chattering away about Malini Mehra. 'Did you see that?' Maya said. 'Of course,' said the woman, 'Malini Mehra likes reds, they suit her skin, don't you think?' Maya looked away again, but the Tetrahedron was just as before. Turning back she met the eyes of the old woman knitting in the doorway of the white van. The old lady smiled at her. Maya wondered if the woman had seen the crow vanish into the Tetrahedron...

Later she met Samir at the tea-shop. He did not ask her where she had been the past three days. It was a relief to sit with him and watch old Ramu boil the tea in a battered saucepan over a kerosene stove. He added a thick pinch of powdered tea and cardamom to the simmering mixture of water and milk. The aroma filled her nostrils. Ramu's radio, tuned to a station that played only classic Hindi film songs, sat perched on the stained wooden counter.

She told Samir about what she had seen.

'I know I wasn't quite close enough to see clearly if the crow did disappear. But so many strange things have happened, no?'

Samir was looking at her thoughtfully. As he started to answer, a sleek grey car stopped in the road across from them. A bright, confident, charming face leaned out of the back window, radiating ethnic chic—from the casually scooped up hair to the embroidered collar of what was probably a very expensive designer salwaar-kameez.

'Bhaiya, don't forget to be on time tonight!'

Bhaiya—Elder brother. Samir waved and looked faintly embarrassed. 'My sister,' he said apologetically as the car drove off in a puff of dust. 'It's her birthday today.'

It occurred to Maya suddenly that Samir was from a quite different stratum of society than herself. She had known this all along—he lived in Greater Kailash, after all, probably in one of those obscenely big houses—but it had never mattered, never seemed important, until now. His English was polished, hers just fluent enough to get by. She remembered meeting a friend of Samir's on their way to the tea-shack some days ago, and the way the friend had looked at her and then again at Samir with astonished surprise. Samir hadn't introduced her. The friend had smiled at Samir and dug him in the ribs and muttered something to him before sauntering off. Something about fraternizing with the vulgar proles? Words she only half caught and did not understand. After that Samir had kept talking to her as though nothing had happened, but just for a fleeting moment he had looked discomfited... Abruptly Maya was aware of herself as hopelessly lower-middle-class, belonging to the petty-tradesmen-uncultured bhainji sub-culture with all its implications. She didn't know anything about Samir's life, nor he about hers—what was she doing here with him?

But he was talking on, oblivious.

'…and maybe it was nothing, but maybe, just maybe, you've hit on something here. There's been a lot of speculation about this. Look,' he drew out his notebook and tore off two pages. He tore one into a rough disk and put it against the edge of the other sheet, at right angles.

'Suppose you were a two-dimensional creature living on the surface of this rectangular sheet of paper. Would you know that this disk existed? No, because it is in the third dimension, right, which is not accessible to you. You would only see the straight line that is the intersection between the disk and the sheet where you exist.'

She concentrated, pushing back her other thoughts.

'Achha, so if I put the edge of my hand against my face,' she said, doing so, 'my face feels only the edge. It has no idea of the extent or shape of my hand.'

'Yes, something like that. You see, it may be that the Tetrahedron is only a projection of a more complicated object in our three-dimensional world. This object extends in a dimension that is inaccessible to us—all we perceive is the Tetrahedron. To us it appears closed. But in another dimension, there may be doors…'

He stopped, lost in thought. Maya was fascinated.

'You mean that somehow the crow I saw got through into another dimension, got into the Tetrahedron? But...'

He took a sip of his tea and set the glass down on the edge of the bench.

'Do you know what topology is?'

She shook her head.

'Simply put, it's a branch of mathematics that concerns itself with very general, basic properties of objects or spaces. Topologists look at what happens if you continuously deform the space or the object without breaking or tearing it... Here, let me give you an example.'

He held the page he had torn from his book in one hand, and the paper disk in the other.

'This rectangular page and this disk of paper are topologically identical, because you can shrink or stretch one to become the other. And your chai glass is identical to them both because I can theoretically deform the sides until it's flat. But—'

He tore a small hole in the middle of the page.

'Now this is no longer topologically equivalent to the disk, because by the rules of topology, however much you deform this page, you can't get rid of the hole. So the page without the hole is a simply connected two-dimensional surface, and the page with the hole is what we call multiply-connected...'

'Oh… Like a teacup… I mean one with a handle, not Ramu's chai glasses.'

'Yes, yes,' he smiled delightedly at her, immensely pleased. 'Topologically you and I are identical to a teacup, or a vada, if you like South Indian food—the human alimentary canal is the analogue of the hole in the vada!'

She was staring at him, wide-eyed. 'Achha, but what has all this to do with—'

'The Tetrahedron? Plenty. Topology is relevant in two ways. One, if the topological structure of the Universe is non-trivial, multiply connected in several dimensions, then it might provide shortcuts for faster-than-light travel. Like the wormholes in space that the newspapers keep talking about. Two, the true shape or structure of the Tetrahedron itself. If we could see it completely in all the dimensions that it inhabits, we might see something topologically very complicated. It would be incomprehensible to us— our notions of in and out, edge and surface would be lost, or at least very confused. Ever seen a Mobius strip?'

She shook her head, feeling awed and small before the vastness of his knowledge. Now what was he doing? His hands, brown and slender—she'd never noticed before how nice his hands were—tore a strip of paper from the long edge of the page. His eyes were alight with enthusiasm.

'Look at this strip of paper—see how I can put the ends together to form a ring?' He suited the action to the word.

'Now suppose, before I do that, I twist the paper once, like this. Now I put the ends together. A ring with a twist! This is a Mobius strip.'

She put a tentative finger out to touch it. He smiled.

'Go on, move your finger along the outer surface, along the length of it... yes, just so!' He grinned at her surprise. 'You start at the outer surface and before you know it, you are inside! Except that inside and outside have lost their meaning in this case, because a Mobius strip has only one surface, not two like the ring.' He was talking fast in his excitement. 'People think that space-time may be a generalization of a Mobius strip or some similar non-trivial topological object, in several dimensions... So also an object like the Tetrahedron could be very complex, very interesting, if we could see it in its entirety...'

Words failed her. She imagined a complicated structure with smoothly contoured edges and sculptured pathways curving dizzily, leading to hidden doors. She stared at him in wonder and envy.

'Hanh, I understand the idea... I think.'

He nodded approvingly.

'If the Tetrahedron is a projection in our space of a more complicated, multi-dimensional object, it might also explain the disappearance of the people who were on the road at the time the Tetrahedron appeared. Who knows?'

'You mean they might be inside the Tetrahedron?'

she said incredulously. The thought had never occurred to her. Instead she had imagined that perhaps some kind of exchange had taken place, the Tetrahedron for the people. That the bus riders, the car passengers and the bicyclists were at this very moment in some other world, walking about under alien skies with their mouths open. Another world! Her mind had conjured up bizarre vistas. Yet the thought of what the inside of the Tetrahedron might be like was equally mind-boggling.

Maya sat talking to Samir for another hour. He told her about current theories of the birth of the universe, the mysteries that arose with each new discovery. She liked the way he gesticulated in his excitement, the way his eyes seemed to see the wonders his words described. Now he was expounding on the eventual death of the universe.

'The solar system, of course, will die long before that,' he said. 'The sun will swell and swallow the earth, the moon, all the nearer planets, before collapsing into a white dwarf star.'

He stopped to take a sip of his tea, and suddenly the radio started playing an old Hemant Kumar favourite: '*Na yeh chand hoga, na taare rahenge...*' *The moon will be no more, nor will the stars remain...*

They both laughed at the same time.

'I have always wondered how in Bollywood films they contrive to have a song with the right words come on at the appropriate moment,' he said, smiling. 'Just the other day a similar coincidence happened. There I was, wondering about what kind of star the aliens are from, if they are aliens, that is, and Ramu's radio started playing *"Chand ke paas jo sitaara hai!"' That star by the moon…*

'Oh yes, that is Lata Mangeshkar and Kishore Kumar,' Maya said. 'I love old film songs. I think Ramu's radio is tuned to the aliens' favourite station!'

It was very pleasant to be able to laugh companionably with somebody. (Maya wondered with a pang whether she and Kartik would ever have anything to laugh about.) Then she remembered fragments of a conversation she had overheard.

'It is syn…synchronicity,' she said carefully. He looked amused.

'That's a big word. Not a scientifically valid concept, of course, but…wasn't it in one of the papers? Where did you come across it?'

'I heard it somewhere.' She felt a slight indignation. What did he think—that she was hopelessly ignorant? Then she thought, depressingly, that it was true.

But Samir was getting up, setting his glass down on Ramu's counter with a rather awkward air.

'Got to go,' he muttered. He looked shyly at her, as though seeing her for the first time. 'See you tomorrow!'

She didn't understand until the radio sang the refrain

again. '*Na yeh chand hoga, na taare rahenge, magar ham hamesha tumhaare rahenge…*' *The moon will be no more, nor will the stars remain, yet I will always be yours…*

She stood staring after him, her face hot with embarrassment. She hoped he didn't think—surely he didn't?

~

When Maya came home one evening, her sister and mother were talking about a story on the afternoon news about a mental sickness that the tabloid press had nicknamed Tetra-fever.

'Isn't it terrible, Maya, there are these people who are obsessed with the Tetrahedron, they can't eat or sleep or function normally—they dream about it all the time,' her sister said, setting a plate of hot onion pakoras before Maya. 'Some of them starve themselves almost to death, there is this fellow being kept alive in a hospital, fed through a tube…' Maya nearly choked over her tea, then took an extra-large helping of the pakoras. Her mother nodded.

'Yes, yes, they talked on TV about a man who stopped going to work, lost his job. He spends all his time staring at the Tetrahedron. He has three children! Poor things, such a terrible thing to happen. At least your father is a sensible man. And there's this housewife, can you imagine, goes shopping at the plaza every day, has the largest collection of plastic tetrahedrons in the city, chee chee!'

Maya nodded, mouth full, and took another pakora.

'Still,' said her mother, pouring herself more tea and liberally adding sugar, 'it is all in God's hands.' She sighed, and Maya knew what she was going to say.

'Nothing to do with us.'

Her father came in at the door, stooping, tired from a long day of work and the hot, sweaty bus ride. Maya felt guilty. Maybe I am one of the crazies, she thought to herself, thinking of all the time she spent away from class, with Samir or at the Tetrahedron. Thank goodness Kartik was out of town... If only her brother, Manoj, was here! She had written to him some time ago but he was on a ship, and his reply would take time. Besides, letters were no substitute for seeing him face to face.

But at least she was able to talk to Samir about the Tetrahedron. Their mutual embarrassment had been short-lived; at their next meeting, they were comfortable with each other again. There was so much to talk about that she no longer paid any attention to Ramu's radio. However, Samir had not been very interested in the occupants of the white van. On a visit to Patel Chowk, he had looked them over rather dismissively—they were not a fascinating astronomical phenomenon after all. He did remark on the old woman knitting away—she was like

Madam Defarge, he said, a character from some famous book she'd never heard of. She found this evidence of his class and education annoying, but at least he did not think she was crazy.

They talked about the latest development in the saga of the Tetrahedron. A man had been found wandering in the Thar desert a few hundred miles west of New Delhi. He had been pushing a bicycle over the sand dunes, a strange sight indeed for the villagers who found him. They related that the man did not seem to know where he was going. Upon being questioned he had replied in what seemed to be gibberish, or another language. He seemed happy enough to be led to a villager's hut, where he had been fed and housed for several days. A social worker had come across him and, based on the contents of a bag strapped to his bicycle, had gathered that he was from New Delhi and contacted the police there. It had finally been established that he was one of the people missing when the Tetrahedron had first appeared.

As could be expected, this caused a sensation. Search teams were sent to comb the Thar desert, and there an astounding discovery had been made. The missing bus had been found in a sandy valley, with fifteen people in it—eleven of the original bus passengers, and four people who had been in cars when the Tetrahedron appeared. All fifteen were alive and well, physically that is. But two of them were in the same state as the bicyclist, and the rest kept eerily silent, reacting to nothing and nobody, confounding doctors and family members alike. Meanwhile the bicyclist's family—he was a postal clerk—appeared on TV expressing relief that he had been found, and hope that he and the others would be cured of their strange malady. The tabloid press had a field day. Headlines across the world proclaimed, '16 People Kidnapped by Aliens Free—But What Happened to Them?'

Maya and Samir could only speculate. As they sat drinking tea, a thought struck Maya.

'The world is like a cracked egg,' she said. 'Our world, I mean, where we live. Everything we know and see and understand is in this egg. But the cracks tell us that there are things outside—a world outside our understanding...'

Samir gave her a startled look.

'You sound quite poetic,' he said, smiling. He cleared his throat, as though to say something. Maya shook her head. An idea had been nagging her for some time, and she had suddenly found the words for it.

'What if the Tetrahedron isn't a spaceship? What if it is something we can't even imagine, something totally unknown? You know, what bothers me about all this is that there is so much talk. Just talk. You scientists seem so sure about one theory or another—but how can you be really know something without any experience of it?'

'That's where experiments come in,' Samir said patiently, ready to expound.

'No, that's not what I mean,' she said. She grinned. 'The other day when you were holding your cup of tea and you told me about what the tea was made of, atoms and molecules, remember? You said if we could understand the smallest constituents of matter, we would be able to know everything there is to know about tea.'

'Well?'

'You forgot to drink it. Your theories can tell you a lot about tea, but not about the experience of drinking it. That is what I mean. I don't have the words to explain it, but…do you know what I mean?'

She was conscious of his gaze suddenly, and it seemed that there was something faintly wistful about it. He hadn't been listening to her. Embarrassed, she began to talk at once about something else that had occurred to her.

'You know, if the idea about the Tetrahedron being what was it—a projection of a larger object in another dimension—if that is true, then maybe this object is huge— so huge that it extends all the way to the Thar desert…'

He raised his eyebrows.

'Hanh, that is possible. Yes, perhaps there is another door somewhere in the Thar where they let them off. But what about the rest of the people who vanished?'

'Maybe they don't want to come back, who knows.

Maybe the aliens are nicer to them than humans are to each other. Maybe this and maybe that. Samir, what I'm trying to say is, how can we know anything about the Tetrahedron without ever having been in it?'

'It isn't as though we haven't tried,' he said a little defensively. 'We've gone over every square centimetre…'

'Would you, if you could?' she interrupted. 'If you found a way, would you go in? Go off on a journey through space?'

'Of course I would!'

He fell silent, rubbing his chin. He gave her an unexpectedly awkward look, then looked away.

'Listen, Maya… I'd like to go inside the Tetrahedron, of course, to study it. But I would have to be sure I could come back. You know,' now he looked at her directly again, but it was a very different kind of look, 'I am very attached to my family… They've been wondering why I've been spending so much time here. My friends, too. They don't always understand me, but still…family is family, don't you think?'

He was looking at her meaningfully, his brown eyes sorrowful, and still she did not understand. Then suddenly she realized what he was saying, what he must think of her and the direction their relationship might be going. Young men and women didn't fraternize one-on-one for weeks on end unless there was some intention, some basis for a very different kind of relationship. Through the host of confused thoughts in her mind, her pride rose like a sword unsheathed.

'I am close to my family too,' she said a little too hurriedly. 'In fact I am engaged to this really nice fellow, Kartik, you must meet him some day…'

He was staring at her, open-mouthed. She couldn't be sure whether he was angry or upset or both. Her face burned. How dare he presume? Their friendship had been strictly in the context of the Tetrahedron—she had expected no more from him than that… Well, yes, she liked him, the way he thought about things, his generosity, the kindness in his eyes, the fact that he didn't automatically assume she was stupid, oh and his hands, how they moved when he was describing something—and yet he had assumed. How could he think her so callow, so simple, like a heroine from a third-rate movie? She wanted to tell him: Yes, my father is a clerk and my mother works in a tailoring shop, but I have a sense of dignity. And, she wanted to say, if we *were* really interested in each other in that way, so what? Coward, getting cold feet before anything had begun! She couldn't trust herself to speak. Angry tears pricked at the corners of her eyes. To hell with you and your expensively dressed-up sister and those snobbish friends you never introduce me to, she told him silently. He was getting up, looking at his watch, making some excuse. He had a class very soon. And some exams coming up... he was going to be very busy from now on. He gave her an uncertain, apologetic smile and walked away through the trees and down the street.

On Ramu's radio, Geeta Dutt began to sing '*Na jao saiiyan, chura ke baiiyan...*' *Don't leave, beloved, stealing my heart away.* She looked at the old man suspiciously. He winked, shrugged his shoulders and went back to scrubbing the counter, a pointless task, she thought inconsequentially, since it always seemed to be dirty.

The next day she did not go to the university. She went straight to Patel Chowk and stood watching the crowd. A crow watched Maya from the roof of the souvenir stall. 'What do you see?' she asked it in her mind. 'What do you see when you look at the Tetrahedron?' The bird cocked its head and stared at her with beady eyes. It gave a caw that sounded like raucous laughter, then took to the air, flapping its wings heavily. Maya sipped her drink and sighed. She saw the old lady in the white van, watching her in a benign sort of way. On an impulse she went up to her.

'What are you knitting?' she asked in Hindi. The old woman looked puzzled. Maya asked the question again in English.

'Ah! Only a sweater for my grandson.' She spoke with a peculiar accent. 'I'm from Mexico,' she said, smiling.

'Here to see the Tetrahedron?' Maya asked, feeling stupid. What else?

'Si… yes. Three times I make the trip to your country. Much like Mexico, here. Hot desert, mountain, seaside, we have them all.' She smiled enigmatically. 'Also old buildings. Yesterday I see the tall Minar, many tombs.'

'Are you with a tourist group?' Maya asked, wondering what Ravindra Refrigeration had to do with sightseeing.

'Tourist? Tourist, yes. Like to come?'

Maya shook her head, smiling distractedly. 'I have to go…'

'Come see us if you like to come. We here until weekend—Saturday. What's your name? Maya? We have that name too!' She smiled with great pleasure.

Maya waved goodbye and wondered rather miserably what she should do. Go back home? Kartik had written to say he would be back next week. It had been a cold sort of letter—clearly he was expecting her to make amends for her behaviour. She could go to class, for a change. Samir could go jump in a well. With that comforting thought she took the bus to the university. Once there she could not bear the thought of dealing with the inane chatter of her friends. It was a hot day—she walked to Ramu's chai shack, thinking maybe she'd have some nimbu-pani instead of tea. The small open space in front of the shack was deserted. She watched the traffic on the road as she sipped her drink, trying not to think about whether Ramu ever washed the glasses. She tried to push away bitter thoughts of Samir. She would miss his friendship—and, she had to admit, the possibilities their relationship had contained. Lata Mangeshkar began singing on the radio: '*Aaj koi naheen apna, kise gham ye sunaayen...*' *Today I have no one to call my own, to whom shall I tell my sorrow...*

Irritably she looked at Ramu but he had his back to her, doing something industrious with a rag. You go jump in a well too, she told him silently. Moisture beaded her glass of nimbu pani. She wiped sweat off her forehead with a handkerchief her mother had embroidered, and found a sudden lump in her throat. It's not just space and time, she thought bitterly, that are multiply connected. If she could talk to Samir now, she'd tell him: outer space, inner space, both have unknown topologies. You couldn't overlook one at the expense of the other. But he wouldn't talk to her anymore, curse him...

On Friday night she was unable to sleep. A pale wash of streetlight lit the room. On the other bed her sister lay sleeping, her arm about Chanchal, who stirred fitfully in a dream. Maya went up to the window and sat on the sill, leaning against the grillwork. Down on the street a watchman banged his stick on the sidewalk as he passed. There was a light on here and there among tiers of darkened windows; she wondered what was keeping those people awake. She thought about the Tetrahedron, dimensional anomalies, synchronicity. The man walking his bicycle in the middle of the Thar desert, the old woman knitting for her grandson, smiling, saying she'd be here till Saturday. Which was tomorrow. In a few days Kartik would be back in Delhi.

Abruptly, everything fell into place. She got up with sudden determination, got the flashlight from her drawer and went softly into the dark drawing room. Carefully she found a sheet of paper, sat in a chair and began to write to Kartik in the dim light of the flashlight, hoping and praying that her parents, in the next room, would not wake up. After she was done she put the letter in an envelope and put a stamp on it. She would mail it tomorrow. She felt a great relief.

Next she wrote a long, affectionate letter to Manoj. 'Try to explain it to them, Bhaiya,' she wrote. 'I don't think I can...'

She went back to the bedroom. Chanchal was awake, crying to go to the bathroom.

'I'll take her,' Maya told her sister, who lay back in sleepy gratitude. Chanchal did her duty and was amiable again. She climbed into bed with Maya. Maya sang to her the old children's song about Uncle Moon, about the child going up in a flying ship to play hide-and-seek among the stars. It was Chanchal's favourite song, and she always asked the same question at the end. 'Will I come back?' Only this time she said, sleepily, 'Will you come back, Maya Mausi?' And Maya said, through her tears, of course I will.

In the morning she rose early, cooked breakfast for everyone and washed the dishes so her mother could rest a while before going to work. She saw off her father at the bus-stop and went to the post-box where she mailed the two letters. Then she took the bus to Patel Chowk, where the white van was parked.

'I will come,' she told the old lady. The woman smiled as though she had always known Maya would.

~

Maya's disappearance on the day the Tetrahedron left New Delhi earned only a small item in the newspapers. What was a missing girl—one of those crazies, to judge from what she had written to her family—what was her absence, compared to the most significant event of the century, the appearance and disappearance of the Tetrahedron? Her family mourned, all except Chanchal, who assured the puzzled grown-ups that Maya would be back. Kartik wrote to say he had always been afraid Maya was a little unstable, and her running away (not to mention the lack of respect in the letter she had written to him) proved it— he considered he had had a narrow escape. If she were found, he hoped the family would punish her suitably for dragging their name in mud. Although they didn't deserve it, he was sending back the little gifts her family had given him. Maya's parents wept over the small package he sent—the final end to their dreams for their youngest daughter. Meanwhile, Manoj took leave and came home, torn between grief and hope.

It was one of the hottest days of the season—the square near the Tetrahedron was nearly empty. Even the man selling cold spiced cucumber slices gathered his things and wandered off into the shade, where he sat dozing. A group of bored soldiers watched Maya, the old woman and the others as they walked up to the Tetrahedron. They just wanted to touch it, and they were unarmed, the soldiers said later. They must have wandered off after that, the soldiers said. We weren't really looking. But what really happened was that Maya and her companions went all the way up to the Tetrahedron and turned in a place where she had not known it was possible to turn. It was a kind of narrow corridor and she could still see the soldiers, the white van with Ravindra Refrigeration on it, the driver getting ready to leave. She could still see the hot, dusty square under the neem trees. But also she found herself in a large room which seemed to be made up of walls arranged at impossible angles, like an Escher picture—and the outside world, if it still made sense to talk of outside and inside—the outside world was projected on a plane slanting up from her feet, making her feel giddy. She looked up and she could see the dark of space amid spiral stairways going towards some distant destination; she saw with a shock that there were creatures going up on it, great beings made up of planes and angles and curves that didn't quite fit. Some of them had human-like faces. She turned in wonder to the old woman beside her and stopped with her mouth hanging open.

For the old woman too, had changed. Her face was still the same, but her eyes had grown large and dark, and a succession of crests and ridges rose from her body in great arcs. There were growths dangling from her arms like the appendages of sea-creatures. She smiled at Maya.

Maya drew back. 'You are an alien,' she said.

'No, my dear,' the woman said in chaste Hindi. 'I am who I am. Remember what I told you? Do not expect to understand everything all at once. I will be your guide. But first, take a look at yourself.'

And the old woman took Maya gently by the shoulders and turned her to a silver wall that was opaque and reflective. Maya saw herself. Saw her face, mouth open in shock, her hair streaming around it, the great crenellations and sweeping ridges that rose from her body as gracefully as the plates on a stegosaurus's back. She looked at her two hands, the familiar river-valley of lines and tributaries, and she saw that they were the same as before, and not the same. Other hands branched off her hands, fading off into an infinity of hands, young hands, old hands, smooth and wrinkled. She took a deep, sobbing breath.

'What has happened to me?'

'Nothing. You see yourself as you are in more than three dimensions. Now don't think about it too much. I want you to look around and tell me where you want to go first.'

Around—whatever that meant—was the darkness of space, and stars caught in a thin, delicate mesh. She saw the great rings of Saturn, the shadows of three of its moons like black pimples on its bright face. She saw other planets, dead stars, worlds that drifted in space without suns. And the spiral stairways moved up and up like escalators, vanishing into the fine intricacy of the web.

'Shall we start with something close to home, like the moon?'

'I thought you said this wasn't a spaceship!'

'It is and it isn't. You will get used to not thinking in the old ways, my dear. The categories we are accustomed to on Earth have little meaning here. A square does not have the same meaning for a flat-land person as it does for a three-dimensional one. You'll see.'

Maya took a deep breath. Around her the Universe beckoned. She thought she heard Lata Mangeshkar and Mohammad Rafi on Ramu's radio, singing: 'Chalo Dildaar, chalo, chand ke paar chalo…' Come, beloved, let us fly beyond the moon.

'Let's go further,' she said.

Was that what really happened to Maya? How can we know? All she left behind was a very detailed letter to her brother, and some ideas and theories. Her story came alive from those scribbled pages, but it necessarily came to a stop when she left home. Perhaps in some dimension orthogonal to time and space, it is possible to see what came after, to follow her world-line, to see the post-script to her letter. But caught in the stream of time as we are, all her brother could do was to wait. He thought of all kinds of other scenarios, of spaceships that swept silently through space like owls through night, of aliens and alien languages, and Maya among impossible worlds, her face filled with a softness and yearning, a kind of tender curiosity. He remembered the child she had been, always straining at the barriers, being scolded and cajoled into doing whatever she was supposed to do. She had learned to replace outward defiance with a quiet raging within herself. He thought of her waiting at the bus-stop on that fateful morning before it all began, unaware of the person she would become, the person who would write so passionately in her last letter: 'What if the Tetrahedron is something that is completely beyond our understanding? How can we know it without experiencing it?'

One day, some weeks after the disappearance, Samir climbed the three flights of stairs to the little flat and talked to Manoj rather incoherently about his conversations with Maya. He never doubted that she was out there somewhere in the distance between the stars. He was about to finish his Ph.D, he was going to an observatory in Chile later in the year, he would keep an eye out for her. At this, Manoj laughed a little bitterly. He guessed something from the dazed look in the young man's eyes.

'I'll be watching too,' he said. 'I think if she comes back it will be in the Thar desert.'

'The Thar…why there?'

'She told me about the white van. It said Ravindra Refrigeration, Udaipur, Rajasthan. No such company, by the way, I checked. But my guess is that was where the Tetrahedron used to appear, in the middle of the desert. This time they made a mistake—or something—who knows? Although there was, I think, at least an exit door still over the Thar…'

Samir ran his fingers through his hair.

'But what does it all mean?' he cried.

He took his leave and returned to campus. He had an appointment with his professor in twenty minutes, and a class to attend after that. It was a hot, still, dusty sort of day, and the grit in the air burned in his throat. He stopped in front of the Physics building, then, abruptly, turned around and made his way to the tea-shack. It was deserted, except for Ramu stirring a potful of aromatic brew. Samir sat down on the bench. Ramu poured out some tea and handed him his glass wordlessly. In the background, the radio was playing an old Kishore Kumar favourite…

'*Chalte, chalte, mere yeh geet yaad rakhana, kabhi alvida na kehena, kabhi alvida na kehena...*' *As you go through life, remember my songs, never say goodbye forever, never say goodbye...*

Samir's eyes filled with tears. In the tree overhead, a crow cawed.

ABOUT THE CONTRIBUTORS

MANJULA PADMANABHAN (b. 1953), is an author, playwright and cartoonist. Her play *Harvest* won the 1997 Onassis Award for Theatre. Her weekly comic strip *Sukiyaki* appears in *Business Line*, in Chennai, India. Her two most recent novels, *Escape* and *The Island of Lost Girls*, are set in a brutal future world. She lives in the US, with a home in New Delhi.

SRINATH PERUR is the author of *If It's Monday It Must Be Madurai*, a book about travelling with groups, and the English translator of the Kannada novel *Ghachar Ghochar*.

JERRY PINTO is a writer who often wonders why it seems he has written more notes about himself than stories. He lives in a city by the sea.

ZAC O'YEAH is a Swedish detective novelist and author of the *Majestic Trilogy*, which is set in his Indian hometown Bengaluru, about the crafty private investigator Hari Majestic. He has published fifteen books, including several fiction and non-fiction bestsellers. His Gandhi biography *Mahatma!* was ranked as the best non-fiction book in Sweden in 2008. His travel writings have appeared in magazines such as *National Geographic Traveller*, *Outlook Traveller*, *RES* and *Vagabond*, and have also been included in many anthologies. All in all he has written for more than seventy-five different publications, including the *Times of India*, *Indian Express*, and *New Indian Express,* amongst others. He is a columnist with the *Business Line* newspaper and a frequent contributor to *The Hindu*. His writings have been translated into German, French, Norwegian, Danish, Finnish, Russian, Chinese and Kannada. He is a founder-director of Bangalore's World-Famous Semi-Deluxe Writing Programme, the first semi-professional writing school in India. His most recent books include the novel *Tropical Detective* and the travelogue *A Walk Through Barygaza*.

RASHMI RUTH DEVADASAN is a founding editor of Blaft Publications. She is the author and imagineer of the picture book *Kumari Loves a Monster* and the playwright of *Ms. Meena* (an adaptation of *The Visit* by Friedrich Dürrenmatt.)

JAGDISH CHANDRA BOSE (1858–1937) was a polymath, physicist, biologist, biophysicist, botanist and archaeologist, and an early writer of science fiction in Bengali. His books include *Response in the Living and Non-Living* (1902) and *The Nervous Mechanism of Plants* (1926).

BODHISATTVA CHATTOPADHYAY is Senior Researcher at the Department of Culture Studies and Oriental Languages, University of Oslo, and, in 2018-19, Fellow at the Centre for Advanced Study at the Norwegian Academy of Science and Letters. He is the Series Editor for *Studies in Global Genre Fiction* (Routledge), Editor-in-chief of *Fafnir: Nordic Journal of Science Fiction and Fantasy Research* (Finfar, Finland), and Editor at the *Journal of Science Fiction* (MOSF, Washington, D.C.). Together with his cactus Albert and aloe Charaka, he works on the field of science fiction and the possibility of many different futures. He can be reached at bodhi@bodhisattvac.com

SUNANDO C. is an illustrator and designer based between Bangalore and Kolkata. He is the artist on comics such as *Work Nights* and the upcoming *Memoria*.

INDRAPRAMIT DAS (AKA INDRA DAS) is a writer and editor from Kolkata. He is a Lambda Literary Award-winner for his debut novel *The Devourers* (Penguin India/Del Rey), and has been a finalist for the Crawford, Tiptree and Shirley Jackson Awards. His short fiction has been appeared in publications including Tor.com, *Clarkesworld* and *Asimov's*, and has been widely anthologized. He is an Octavia E. Butler Scholar and a grateful graduate of Clarion West 2012. He has lived in India, the United States, and Canada, where he completed his MFA at the University of British Columbia. You can follow him on Twitter @IndrapramitDas.

SHALINI SRINIVASAN writes children's books, comics, and the occasional bit of academic flimflammery. She lives in Bangalore, and currently spends a lot of time holding forth on grammar at hapless adolescents.

VANDANA SINGH was born and raised in New Delhi, and currently lives in the United States near Boston, where she professes Physics and writes. Her short stories have appeared in numerous venues and several Best of Year anthologies, including the Best American Science Fiction & Fantasy. She is the author of the ALA Notable book *Younguncle Comes to Town* (Young Zubaan/Puffin India; 2004) and a previous short-story collection, *The Woman Who Thought She Was a Planet and Other Stories* (Zubaan/Penguin India; 2009).

EDITOR'S ACKNOWLEDGEMENTS

Thanks to:

Sudeshna Shome Ghosh: for always countering my meltdowns with grace and good cheer.

Radhika Shenoy: for yor keeen editorial eye & ur infnite payteince… --- ##

The authors in this book: for trusting me with your strange and beautiful words/images. You guys are the best.

Yamini: for reading, for believing, and for being.